THE

CRANE

HUSBAND

KELLY BARNHILL

THE

CRANE

HUSBAND

TOR PUBLISHING GROUP  NEW YORK

THE CRANE HUSBAND

A Tordotcom Book
Published by Tom Doherty Associates/Tor Publishing Group
120 Broadway
New York, NY 10271

www.tor.com

Tor® is a registered trademark of Macmillan Publishing Group, LLC.

Library of Congress Cataloging-in-Publication Data

Names: Barnhill, Kelly Regan, author.
Title: The crane husband / Kelly Barnhill.
Description: First edition. | New York : Tor, 2023. | "A Tom
    Doherty Associates book."
Identifiers: LCCN 2022034813 (print) | LCCN 2022034814
    (ebook) | ISBN 9781250850973 (hardcover) | ISBN
    9781250850980 (ebook)
Subjects: LCGFT: Novels.
Classification: LCC PS3602.A777134 C73 2023 (print) |
    LCC PS3602.A777134 (ebook) | DDC 813/.6—dc23/
    eng/20220722
LC record available at https://lccn.loc.gov/2022034813
LC ebook record available at https://lccn.loc.gov/2022034814

Our books may be purchased in bulk for promotional, educational, or
business use. Please contact the Macmillan Corporate and Premium Sales
Department at 1-800-221-7945, extension 5442, or by email at
MacmillanSpecialMarkets@macmillan.com.

First Edition: 2023

Printed in the United States of America

0 9 8 7 6 5 4 3 2 1

To the mothers who flew away.
And to those they left behind.

1.

The crane came in through the front door like he owned the place. My mother walked slightly behind, her hand buried past her wrist in his feathers. He was a tall fellow. Taller than a man, by a little bit. I watched him duck his head down to pass through the low doorway leading into our elderly farmhouse. His stride was like that of any other crane, all dips and angles, forward and back, and yet. He still seemed to carry himself with an unmistakable swagger. He surveyed our house with a leer. I frowned.

I had already set the table and sliced and buttered the bread—it was stale around the edges but so it goes. I did my best to soften it under a warm, damp paper towel for a minute or two. The canned soup bubbled on the stove.

My brother, only six years old at the time, sat perfectly still in his chair, his eyes wide and solemn. He stared at the spindly gait of the crane as it stalked across the sitting room, its long neck hinging with each step, like a metronome. The crane stopped when they reached the threshold to the kitchen. He cocked his head. My mother stood by his side, her hair disheveled, her sweater drifting down the outer curve of her left shoulder. She leaned her head against him. Were they waiting to be invited in? It was her house. She had never hesitated when bringing guests over before.

Granted: this was her first crane.

My brother's mouth fell open.

"Michael," I whispered, "keep your mouth closed." I was fifteen and had been in charge of Michael since he was born. He did as he was told. He trusted me, utterly. Under the table, his small, warm hand found mine and hung on tight. He shut his teeth with a snap but kept his large eyes fixed on the bird.

I stared, too. I couldn't help it. It was an enormous crane. He loomed over my mother, and she was tall to begin with. She gazed up at the crane, who gazed back. She giggled, briefly, like a girl. I pressed my mouth into a grim line. I knew what that giggle meant. She buried her other hand in his feathers, squeezing and releasing her fingers, luxuriating a bit.

"Darlings," my mother said, "I'd like you to meet someone."

The crane wore a man's hat, tipped forward at what I suppose was a jaunty angle. He wore spectacles perched on his beak (razor sharp, I noticed right away). But his eyes— hard and black and keen, and so shiny it almost hurt to look at them—didn't peer through the spectacles at all. I had a suspicion that they were just for show.

He and my mother stepped farther inside. The crane had a broken wing, bound in a splint that looked as though it had been made from two bits of wood and strips torn from one of my mother's shirts. It rested in a sling that had all the hallmarks of my mother's careful construction—intricate stitchwork and the occasional moment of surprising beauty. He attempted to wear shoes, like a man, but his clawed feet had already pierced through the leather and he scratched the floor with each clunk of his footsteps. The shoes, too, were just for show.

(The shoes, I noticed, were my father's. Or had been when my father was alive. Not that I had any memory of my father wearing those shoes. Or any shoes, for that matter. My only memories of him were from his sickroom when he and I would sit for hours playing card games of my own invention, usually with names like "Who's Got the Highest?" or "These Cards Are Now Married and Isn't That Wonderful," during which he would cheerfully let me win. I have only one memory from when he lay on his deathbed, but I do not think of it much.)

The crane spread his good wing around my mother. Right away, I watched as that wing slid down her back and curled over her rump. I must have made a face, because my mother instantly folded her arms and gave me a *look*.

"Is that any way," she said without finishing her sentence.

I shrugged.

Michael said nothing.

"Is he staying?" I asked. I meant for dinner.

"Of *course* he is," my mother said, meaning, I later realized, something else entirely.

The crane tilted his long beak down toward my mother, nuzzling her neck. The sharp tip nipped the well behind her collarbone, making a bright spot of blood. She didn't seem to notice. But the crane did. Or, it seemed to me that

he did. He puffed his feathers in a self-satisfied sort of
way. I frowned. I made another place at the table and
added water to the soup to spread it out among the four of
us. I pulled another bowl out of the cupboard.

"What happened to his wing?" I asked, inclining my
head toward the splint and the sling. The crane flinched
at the mention of it.

"Surely you remember," my mother said, soothingly
running her fingers along the crane's neck and not looking
at me at all.

I shook my head. Why would I remember? But I decided to ignore this. My mom lived in her own head sometimes. Artists are like that, I'm told.

"What are we to call him?" I said, more as a resigna-
tion than a question. "You haven't exactly introduced us."
I rummaged in the drawer for an extra spoon, not wanting
to look at either of them. And, in truth, I didn't particularly care about the answer. I didn't intend to call the crane
anything at all. He'd be gone soon enough anyway. Probably by morning. I don't think my mother had ever kept
anyone around for more than a week, so I never much saw
the point of learning the names of the people she brought
home.

She pulled out the chairs, the legs screeching against
the kitchen floor.

"Sit, my love," she said to him and not to me. I ladled
the soup into bowls and tossed salad greens that I had
grown in the yard and served those, too. I hoped no one
would notice the staleness of the bread. My mother sat
on the crane's lap, her arms draped across his back, her
body obscured by his functional wing. The blood from her
collarbone smeared across his gray feathers. He clucked

and cooed, running his beak along her denimed thighs, picking at the fabric until it frayed.

Michael and I began eating. My mother still hadn't answered the question. Michael kept his eyes tilted toward the table. I don't think he looked up once.

Finally: "Father," she said, her hands on either side of the crane's face, her gaze peering into one black eye. She didn't look at us at all. "You will call him Father."

Fat chance, I thought waspishly.

And even though I knew enough about birds to know that they're not much for facial expressions, there was no mistaking the bird's randy, jubilant smirk. He puffed his feathers and preened. I slurped down my soup and excused myself from the table, saying I had homework to do—which was true, but I had no intention of actually doing it.

He won't last, I told myself. *Of course he won't.* My mother wasn't one to keep anything around, save for me and Michael. So I wasn't particularly worried about the crane.

I should have been worried about the crane.

2.

Later that evening I returned to the kitchen and saw that my mother and the crane had settled themselves into the living room, their bodies wound together and collapsed in a heap at the edge of the sofa. She showed him photo albums of Michael and me when we were little, gushing at how cute we used to be, as if he cared. They whispered and cooed to one another as I did the dishes and scrubbed the kitchen. They didn't even look up. I wiped down the counters pointedly and glared as I left the room.

I helped Michael with his spelling homework and gave him his bath. I read to him and put him in his jammies and kissed him good night. Normally this would be a time when my mother would be at her loom in her studio, finishing a project for a new buyer, or tending to some of the other odd jobs that she did to keep us mostly afloat. But she wasn't doing any of that. She remained on the couch with the crane, a tangle of arms and legs and feathers. At one point she threw her head back and laughed.

"I guess you weren't planning on checking on the animals?" I said, a bite in my voice. "Or locking the gate?" My mother did not acknowledge that I had even spoken. "Or any other damn thing?" I muttered peevishly, before stomping outside, throwing my coat on, in a huff.

I wasn't expecting my mother to follow. I *hoped* she would follow. But she didn't.

The night was dark and the stars were out, so bright and sharp it hurt to look at them. The farm on the other side of the fence was an endless, yawning black, broken every now and again by the occasional blinking light. It was too early for there to be any activity on the farmland to speak of, but the cold light from the eyes of the sentinel drones still slid through the dark fields on the other side of the electric fence. Keeping the land safe from, well, who knows what. It was not my family's farm, after all—at least, not anymore—and it was none of my concern. My mother's father lost the farm when she was still a girl. We still have the house, though. And the barn. And a view over the endless, untouchable fields, a portion of which we once could have called ours.

It was warm for the end of February. The temperature had dipped below freezing, but only just. The dead grass and fence posts sparkled with frost, and the wind moved heavily with a damp chill. Every year, spring came earlier. Soon, people said, there would be no more winter at all.

My mother's studio occupied the entire upper level of the old barn. Most of the lower level we used for storage—odds and ends from when my family used to farm, my mother's first loom, materials for projects, cheese-making supplies. Off to the side was the pen for the sheep, who huddled in a corner and refused to move. Even when I filled their troughs with food, they still wouldn't budge.

Something had spooked them.

"Hey, dummies," I said gently. "What's got you upset?"

The sheep stared at me, their eyes wide and wild. Normally it was my mother who fed them and milked them and ran her hands along their faces until they sighed. She cooed to them and calmed them. She said this was important, that she should maintain a close bond with the sheep since she was the one who would be stealing their wool twice a year, holding them down, her knee on their necks to quell their struggling as she ran the shears, ignoring their screams every time she accidentally nicked their skin. And when our previous sheep couldn't give milk anymore, when their wool became coarse and sparse and unusable, she beckoned them close as she held the knife and held them tenderly as she bled them dry. She wept as she salted their meat, and tanned their skins, and boiled their bones for soup. She said it was a sin to butcher an animal that you didn't love first.

And it was true. She loved the sheep. And they loved her back.

"It's a sad fact about true love," my mother told me once. "The sheep love me without ceasing, and that is why I am able to cause them pain—love is the path of least resistance, you see? It's a lot more work to cause harm to someone who mistrusts you, or fears you. Or hates you. Love opens the city gates wide, and allows all manner of horrors right inside. This is why they don't flinch when I come at them with something unpleasant." She paused for a moment. She took my hand between both of hers and her face became grave. "It's the same thing with us. You'll understand this when you're older. You'll learn that you're safest around the people you mistrust and dislike. Your guard is up, you see? The more you love someone, the more dangerous to you they become. The more you love someone, the more willing you are to show them your throat."

At the time, I thought this was wise. I think differently now.

I climbed into the pen and knelt down next to the sheep. I breathed on their faces. I rubbed their jowls. I fed them from my hands. I spoke softly, kindly, my words filled with love. Just like my mom. Slowly they started to relax. The oldest, a ewe named Nix, sighed a bit and knelt close, resting her chin on my knee, groaning at her protesting joints. Her milk had been waning lately. She was developing bald patches. She wouldn't be around for much longer. I put my arm around her neck, her wool sticky with lanolin funk. I'd need a bath after for sure, but I didn't mind. I tried to slow down my breathing, and after a bit Nix did the same, relaxing even more. Soon the other sheep followed suit.

After several tries, I finally coaxed the three of them to their food bins, and Nix took a couple of cautious nibbles while the other two sniffed. Their nostrils flared. Their eyes kept flicking to the house. They had just begun to munch when the back screen door opened with a loud whine. My mother and the crane stumbled out into the yard as though they were drunk, though my mother didn't drink. Her arms twined around the crane's body, his long neck leaning across her shoulders. She opened her throat and laughed, her voice large in the quiet night. The crane snorted and guffawed like a man.

The sheep bleated and whined. They shied from their food. Shied from the house. They turned away from my mother, even though they loved her. They stamped and shook.

"Let me show you what I made for you, baby," my mother said to the crane. "Let me show you every beautiful thing."

The sheep worried and shivered. Nix was beside herself. Beverly vomited onto the ground. The wind moaned across the empty fields. The stars glinted harsh in the sky. I stayed close to the sheep, trying to quiet them with a still presence. Trying to calm them with quiet breathing.

"What's gotten into you?" I asked.

"Meh," said Nix, her eyes bulging.

I watched as my mother and the crane went through the door to the studio and closed it behind them with a loud slap. I startled. My mother's laughter continued, muffled, from inside. Nix stamped her feet. I gave her neck an appreciative scratch.

"Yeah," I said to the sheep. "I don't like him either."

I put on their hoods and rubbed their noses and kissed each sheep good night.

3.

Our house stood at the very edge of town. It was the last of the old farmhouses, the only one that the conglomerate hadn't knocked over when they bought our farm and the rest of the farms in the area. An electric fence separated our yard from monocultured fields on the other side. Cloned corn in every direction, stretching all the way to the sky. During the summer, the fields hummed and whispered each day. The hum of drones. The surprisingly loud whisper of corn as it grows. Sometimes the whole world rumbled and roared with the sound of the tremendous engines of those driverless tractors and remote-control harvesters. We were not allowed to set foot on those fields—the kids in town who disobeyed that rule ultimately found themselves photographed by the conglomerate's sentinel drones, each equipped with state-of-the-art facial recognition software, and their families were sent stern letters, first with a warning and then with a substantial fine. Our town was situated right where the driftless bluffs descended into plains of ancient glacial silt, and its acres and acres of rich, flat farmland, all tended to remotely by one guy named Horace who kept the whole operation going in a room full of computers and readout machines (and who drank too much on Saturdays). He wasn't a farmer. He was a *technician*. No one was a farmer anymore. No one touched the dirt anymore. No one walked through the endless rows, their fingers whispering along the dark green leaves. No one was allowed—not us, not strangers, not animals. Even the birds weren't allowed. Every day the drones moved back and forth, back and forth, guarding a world made only for corn.

Time was, everyone around here was a farmer, or was married to a farmer, or did business with farmers, or worked for farmers. The kids in town, like Michael and me, were the grandchildren or great-grandchildren of farmers, our families' toil and legacies long since bought, or wagered, or lost. Now no one person owns that land. Except the conglomerate, but that's not really a person, no matter what the law says. The conglomerate was, and is, owned by stockholders, who all live far, far away. Most of them have never seen this place, and I doubt they ever will.

I don't say this to blame them. The world changes, after all.

Our house was lopsided and haphazard in the way that most farmhouses used to be, back in the day, built by hand and with additions tacked on at random, depending on the family's need. I'm not sure which one of my various great-grandfathers built the original structure. I do know that there was a photograph of my grandfather as a little boy, carrying a bucket of tools to his father and grandfather as they built the newest section. I never met my grandfather. Or any of the men that came before him. But I've seen what they looked like—there was a long line of framed photographs of grim-faced men staring out from the wall of the back hallway, which led up to the attic. I avoided that hallway, if I could help it. They weren't . . . *happy* men, the farmers of my family.

When I was young, my mother used to tell me that her father was a hard man, from a long line of hard men. When she said this, her expression became blank, unreadable, and her cheeks, normally taut and ruddy with life and love and creative spark, became dull and slack. This was a temporary phenomenon, and for a long time, I convinced myself that I had merely imagined this change. My mother, in all aspects of her life, was a hungry person. Curious and eager. A whirlwind of making and being and motion. The lifelessness that overtook her face from time to time felt so unnatural, so improbable, that it was easy to tell myself that it couldn't have happened at all.

"But what *made* Granddad a hard man?" I asked her once. "How did he get that way?" I think I was nine. I was sitting with her in her studio as she sketched out image after image for a new tapestry that would soon begin to form on her loom. As she finished, she held each drawing up to the light for a moment, scowling at the details, before crumpling it up in her hands and letting each one fall to the floor. Then she'd start another, and another, her bad mood winding around her body like a shroud. I understood that the pictures she drew were making her unhappy, and that realization made me uncomfortable for reasons I couldn't articulate or process. All I knew was that I didn't like my mother frowning so much.

I had a cozy spot to sit in the corner that my mother had

arranged with cushions and blankets and a soft rug. She also built a shelf for my books. I leaned on a cushion with its riot of patchwork flowers and brightly colored birds that my mother had carefully sewn or embroidered, all layered into a soft cacophony of texture and hue. I attempted to read my book with one hand and solve my Rubik's Cube with the other at the same time. I wasn't doing either of them particularly well.

I don't know why I thought to ask. A vexing dream the night before, perhaps. Or a turn of phrase that suddenly made me curious. Right away, after I asked her, I watched as my mother's shoulders hitched up. She turned her face away from me, showing the length of her slender neck.

Michael, I remember, was an infant and fast asleep in the bassinet in the corner. Every once in a while he grunted or sighed in his sleep. My father was still alive, but only just. His sickroom in our house hummed with machines that monitored his breathing and machines that provided him oxygen and machines that delivered his medicine. A hospice nurse came by every morning to see to my father's body and check in with the family. My mother refused to learn her name.

There were three pictures of my grandfather in the house—one of him as a boy hung in the bathroom; the photo of his wedding day hung in the living room, showing him standing unsmiling next to a beautiful girl half his age; the third hung in the back hallway, along with the long line of men who came before him. In his hallway picture, he was merely a silhouette, dwarfed by the swells of the farm and the unrelenting sky. Even then, as tiny as his figure was, he took a harsh stance. Aggressive shoulders. Hands curled into fists. I didn't like to look at it.

The only man I ever really knew then (and perhaps ever)

was my father. He was a gentle person, and soft. Made softer by illness. I didn't have to have this explained. It was obvious. Everything about my father was soft, from his voice to the tenderness of his hands to the way he turned a phrase. Even now, my memories of him are delicate, like an eyelash on a cheek, or a tiny filament from a cotton-wood tree, resting briefly on the skin.

My mother called her father a hard man, but I honestly couldn't understand what that even meant. So I asked. I waited for my mother to explain it. I waited for a long time.

Finally, she shrugged. "They say that farming made men hard, back when people used to farm. But maybe that's not true. Maybe it was never true. My father was hard when he worked the farm, and hard when he lost the farm, and likely would have been hard in any sort of life. He hated farming until the bank took it away, and then he mourned it terrible. He drank. And raged. And he fought to get the farm back until he couldn't fight it anymore, and then he fought everyone else. Including me. Especially me."

I was quiet for a moment. This wasn't the answer I was looking for. I was, as I said, only nine. But my mother often spoke to me as though I were a peer rather than a child and expected me to understand things for which I did not yet have context. I didn't know then to resent her for it. Instead I changed the subject.

"Daddy's soft," I said because it was true. It was my favorite thing about him. He hadn't gotten out of bed in weeks, and wouldn't, as it turned out, ever again, but I didn't know that yet. And even if I did, I'm not sure it would have mattered in how I understood the world at the time. All I knew was that I loved spending time with him, cocooned in quilts that my mother had sewn and bound by pillows. I loved the briny, waterlogged smell of him, the way his fingertips wrinkled as though he had spent the day in water. I loved the wisps of his shed hair on the pillows, the way his fragile skin hung from his body like cotton curtains in a summer breeze.

"I suppose he is," my mother said. She looked down at her hands. "Very soft."

She went quiet for a moment. I watched her face. She had no expression at all. "On the farm," she said quietly, "mothers fly away like migrating birds. And fathers die too young. This is why farmers have daughters. To keep things going in the meantime, until it's our time to grow wings. Go soaring away across the sky."

I stood. My mother straightened in her chair, lengthened her spine, her long neck stretching prettily in the direction of the window, smiling vaguely at the sky. Her face was wistful. It bothered me that it was wistful. She curled her hand across her mouth. I walked over to her desk and peered at what she was drawing. She had several versions of the same idea—a woman standing in a field looking up. She held a child's hand with one hand and held a baby in the crook of her arm. She was standing in what looked like a pile of leaves, but on closer inspection they were actually feathers. And on the woman's face, my mother had drawn two stitched X's where the eyes should be. I shuddered and looked away.

"But not you, Mom," I said. "You wouldn't fly away." I had a strange and unpleasant feeling that I did not know how to identify. Like my skin was too tight and the air in my lungs had vanished. Like my muscles were suddenly attacked by a thousand tiny thorns. I swallowed with difficulty. "You *wouldn't* leave us, right? Because you need to take care of us. And Daddy. And anyway, there's no farm anymore. Not for us. It's on the other side of the mean fence, and it's somebody else's now. What would you even fly away from?"

Her face crumpled. I didn't understand why. She looked back at her drawings. "I suppose you're right," she said without looking up. "There's no farm at all." And she went back to her work.

I had nightmares after that. I dreamed of my mother standing in the endless fields beyond our yard, where no one was allowed to go, wings erupting from her bloody back, feathers piercing and rustling their way out of her skin, her beaking mouth open in a scream at first, then a sigh, then a bright keen as she lifted skyward and flew away.

My father died a month later. And I was terrified of being alone.

4.

Michael came into my room the night the crane arrived, long after I had put him to bed.

I also should have been asleep. Instead, I sat at my desk, drawing pictures, again, of my father. I drew him sitting at the dinner table, or digging in the garden, or climbing a tree. There were drawings of my father fixing a fence, or driving a truck, or carrying Michael on his shoulders, or doing any one of a myriad of tasks that I never once saw him doing in life. I had boxes of them. I never showed them to my mom.

Michael opened the door silently and pushed it shut without as much as a whisper. I don't know how long he stood there, just staring at me, but when I turned to stretch, he scared me so much I nearly jumped.

"Shhh," Michael said.

"What on *earth* are you doing up?" I asked. I looked at the clock. It was one in the morning. The headboard in my mother's room thumped against the wall. I shuddered.

Michael shouldn't be hearing this, I thought. I tried to admonish him into going back to bed. "And *what are you doing in my room*?" I demanded.

"There's something wrong," Michael said. His large brown eyes were slicked with tears.

"Everything's fine," I said. "And normal. Mom just . . ." I tried to find a sentence that could possibly be useful to a six-year-old. I frowned and pressed on. "Mom has . . . good friends sometimes. But not for very long. They are sometimes-friends. You don't have to like them because they go and find . . . other friends. Later." This wasn't going well. My cheeks felt hot and red. My voice faltered as I continued. "You know. In a regular way. They find new friends later. Some friends are just like that."

Michael shook his head. He looked back toward the hallway. My mom made a low cry. And the crane made a grunt that sounded a lot like a man. *Gross,* I thought.

"He's hurting her," Michael said, hiccuping slightly.

I shook my head, wanting to strangle my mother. She was never entirely discreet when she had a new bedfellow, but this was out of bounds even for her. I was only fifteen. I shouldn't've had to explain the concept of casual sex to my baby brother. That was my *mom's* job.

I knelt down next to Michael and hugged him tight.

"Look," I said. "I get it. This stuff can be very confusing. But I promise you that Mom is better than anyone else in the whole world at taking care of herself. Nobody's hurting anyone. They're just—" There was another enthusiastic groan from my mother's room. Flushed and furious, I shut my bedroom door. "You know what, buddy? Just don't worry about it. How about you sleep in my room tonight? A sleepover. It'll be fun." And that's what we did, with

Michael tucked into the curl of my body like a tiny pearl in the shell of an oyster.

That night, I dreamed that Michael was a fish in a pond, swimming madly in its escape from the relentless thrust of a razor-sharp beak. At the last moment, there was nowhere to hide. The tip of the beak reached the tiny curve of his belly. I woke with a strangled scream.

"You're holding me too tight," Michael murmured in complaint. He was right. My arms had wrapped around his body like a vise.

"Sorry, buddy," I said, releasing him. We were both soaked with sweat—mine, probably. And my heart still raced. "Let's go back to sleep," I whispered.

He did; I didn't. I didn't want to have that dream again. Within moments, Michael was snoring and I got up to stand by my window, as I tried to calm myself down. I pressed my forehead to the glass and squinted. There was a man outside, naked, creeping along the edge of the pond, moving in and out of shadow, his bare feet padding across the frost-touched grass. *Not another one,* I thought scathingly, shaking my head. *Haven't these people heard of frostbite?* His arm was in a sling. The moon shone on his bare skin. He knelt at the edge of the pond and reached his hands through the fragile skin of new ice into the dark, cold water and began rooting around, as though searching for something in the mucky bottom. I blinked and looked at my clock, just as it switched from 2:59 to 3:00. I looked back at the figure in the yard. It wasn't a man at all. It was the crane. I shook my head, trying to clear it. I looked again. It was definitely just the crane. It swung its beak back into the water and tossed a small something into its throat. A frog, maybe. Or a very small fish. I shivered.

It was too late at night to think clearly. I stepped away from the window and pressed my hands against my face, grounding my senses. I listened to myself breathe for a moment.

"He'll be gone soon," I whispered, as though saying it out loud would make it happen faster. And I slid back into bed next to Michael.

5.

The town where I grew up is one of those places in the Midwest that still mostly looks the same as it did a hundred years ago—not because of anyone's particular effort, but rather because there wasn't much reason to grow or change. Instead, from the time of its founding on forward, it has remained fixed in place, like a butterfly pinned to a board, left under glass for so long that eventually it becomes no more than husk and faded color and collapsing dust. There were two historic inns that serviced the tourists who would arrive each spring to admire the blossoms adorning our crab apple and cherry and plum trees, and would return each fall to pay their respects to the elderly maples and oaks, with their yearly displays of vivid color. They admired the charming storefronts and the quaint gazebo in the adorable town square, never really noticing the peeling paint or the sagging roofs or the missing bricks in the walkways. They drove their cars too fast on the winding roads through the bluffs. Once a year, the suited executives from the farming conglomerate descended on the town and took up residence in the inns during their leadership meetings, when they would gaze out on the monocultured fields and pretend that they were still connected to the land. They imagined themselves in overalls and scuffed boots and wide-brimmed hats. They imagined sunburned necks and dirt under the fingernails and the caw of crows circling over the fields. Then they would gorge themselves on local beers and local cheeses and help themselves to lavish platters purported to be grown from local gardens—though, in truth, much of the produce was simply trucked in from greenhouses in the city. The beer, too, mostly.

There were a lot of executives at these meetings, all polished shoes and PowerPoints and loud guffaws. And they ate an astonishing amount. It was good for business in town, having rich strangers arrive regularly. They were hungry for authentic, transcendent experiences. And my mother was happy to provide.

My mother was known for a lot of things back then. Her art, for one. She wove tapestries using gathered fibers and found materials (along with the wool from our three sheep), stitching them into outlandish and multidimensional images and stories. They were massive, my mother's tapestries, and beautiful. Even I could see that. Collectors came from all over to see what she had made. Every time, they stood, rooted to the ground, their mouths open, their hands on their hearts. Once, I saw a woman burst into song. Another time, a man pulled out his phone and apologized to every person he had ever wronged—including my mother, for the sins he had thought about but had not yet committed. Often, I saw collectors fall to their knees and weep. My mother took all of this in stride. She always found ways to make her admirers feel better, up in her studio in the loft of the old barn. Sometimes she made them feel better for hours. I didn't ask any questions about that.

She was also known for her cheese, which she sold to local establishments, and at her stall at the farmers market, and sometimes to vendors far away in the city. She made small batches from carefully guarded recipes, never increasing the size of her operation. The cheese was a side hustle that kept food on the table in between art sales. She called her cheese local and put "100% local" on the label, but in truth there weren't very many dairy farmers left in the county—a dying breed, as they say—and I'm sure by now they're all wiped out. Instead, she bought her milk in bulk from brokers in Canada or California or Mexico, or even China—it arrived periodically in slushy barrels—which she then fortified with powder and amended with milk from our sheep. I fussed at her for the ethics of this but she shrugged it off. "Who cares if the milk's not 100 percent local?" she told me. "*I'm* five generations local. That's enough local for anyone. All people really care about is that it's made in a barn. Or next to a barn. I don't know why that matters, but it does." There was nothing more to say, so I just helped her press the curds.

My mother was also known for taking in strays. Dogs. Cats. Red-tailed hawks. Fox kits and rabbits and wandering goats and, every once in a while, an extremely lost ferret. Once she took in a beautiful, multicolored, and grievously injured pheasant, who took up residence in the well of her lap, luxuriating in the smell of her and curling into her arms. My mother did her best to make the pheasant comfortable—dressing wounds and providing delicacies to nibble on and letting the bird rest his head on her chest.

The pheasant stayed in my mother's arms for three days before he died, whereupon my mother took him out back, plucked him, gutted him, and baked him with onions. She was a farmer's daughter, after all, and nothing if not ruthlessly practical. And anyway, the bird was delicious.

Her lovers were strays as well. A metalworker from two counties over, fired for drinking on the job, waiting for his buddy to roll into town so they could both look for work out west. A shrill soprano who sang show tunes at one of the inns during the tourist season. A street performer who had been grossly misinformed about the interest and generosity of the tourist population during the summertime. An actual vagabond with a tattoo of every town where he had slept rough (ink covered him). The philandering chef at one of the local restaurants who had been kicked out by her wife. Men, women, and those who had transcended those categories entirely, my mother took them all, and delighted in them all.

They didn't stay.

My mother wasn't one for settling down, since Dad died. Not anymore. Or so I thought.

Before the crane arrived, a man had appeared, briefly, in our home. It was late at night—midnight, I think, or maybe further into the wee hours—and Michael was asleep. Mom and I had gone outside to watch the Quadrantid meteor shower. It was January and weirdly warm. The whole world was warm. The deep freezes and wide snowfields that my mother remembered from her youth had transformed to winters that now oscillated between unsettlingly temperate damp and bitter cold.

That particular January consisted of miserable drizzle and wind during the day, and nights that were just cold enough to firm up the mud, each night making new ice crystals that scattered across the yard like stars. We wore wool sweaters and wool hats and our breath lingered in front of our mouths, like ghosts. We had only just spread out our blanket when we heard the sound of a man whimpering in the dark.

"Stay here," my mother said as she stood, her voice terse and vigilant, but I didn't. I followed her as she followed the voice. We found a man sprawled in the sheep pen, injured and groaning. He had deep gashes on his shoulders and on his left thigh and bruises nearly everywhere else. His swollen arm had a bulge where the bone had snapped. He was also entirely naked.

He didn't seem to mind the cold. It didn't look like he noticed it at all.

"Well," he said, looking down at the whole of himself, a tiny smile buried in his mask of pain. "This is embarrassing." He made no move to cover up.

My mother was unfazed. "Darling," she said to me without so much as a turn of her gaze, "go get the blanket." She didn't take her eyes off the man.

His sheepish grin revealed two bloody gaps where his teeth no longer rooted. There were feathers strewn across his body. And feathers drifting across the yard. A pile of feathers in the sheep pen. The sheep wouldn't go near them.

My mother didn't notice the feathers.

"What happened to you?" my mother asked.

The man shrugged. "My own fault really. Had a run-in with one of those damn drones on that farm over there. Nasty buggers. And rude. But I suppose it does serve me right for swerving over those fields. I guess I should have known better."

I frowned. The drones fly. Their purpose—in addition to warding off intruders with their electric eyes and facial recognition software—was to keep the crows out of the corn and send alerts when they detected that the moles had taken it into their heads to start digging. But they stay far above the height of a person—it's one of their rules. So he couldn't have meant a *farm* drone, could he? Maybe he meant the autopiloted tractors. But they weren't even out this time of year. I folded my arms and pressed my skepticism into my face.

My mother had the opposite reaction.

"Oh!" she said. "You poor man!" She helped him to his feet and wrapped him in the blanket and let him drape his weight over her as she assisted him into the house. I followed, noting the trail of feathers he left in his wake. I had no idea where they were even coming from.

Inside the house, my mother, ever the seamstress, sterilized needles and stitched his wounds shut. Growing up on the farm (and with a drunk for a father), she knew a thing or two about the precision needed to neatly sew gaping skin, as well as how to properly set a bone. She gave him a large glass of whiskey and told him to close his eyes and relax. He buried his face in her abdomen and hooked his good arm around her hips and hung on tight. She gripped his wrist and steadied his bicep and pulled, sure and quick. The bone made a deep thumping sound as it righted itself. He howled with pain and relief and wept into her shirt. She went to the wood shop in the basement to fashion two paddles to make a splint. She sang to him as she wound the bandage around his arm and poured him another whiskey.

He had a wildness about him—a feral leer. He watched my mother like she was food and he hadn't eaten in years.

That night, he demonstrated his gratitude in my mother's room. The whole house shook. I put headphones over my ears and listened to foreign broadcasts on my father's old shortwave radio, trying to remind myself that there was a wider world outside of my mother's yard.

There were five stray animals living in our house then. Two cats, a recuperating mourning dove, and a nesting pair of wood ducks. They made themselves scarce that night. This wasn't entirely unusual—strays wander in and wander out, after all. But they never returned. Not a single one. Not after I set out their food on the stoop and left a window open for them to crawl back in. I had never seen our animal guests behave like that.

The next morning the house was filled with feathers and the man was gone. It wasn't the first time one of my mother's visitors left before the sun rose. Normally, she carried on with her day, still flushed from the thrill of the night before, and focused on the work ahead of her. But this was different. She was tearful and quiet. She stood at the window, her fingers wound up in yarn and busily making small figures out of knots. A man made of knots. A woman made of knots. A sigh rattled in the back of her throat. She kept her eyes on the sky. I cooked breakfast and did the dishes. I tried to get her to eat, but it was no use. Quietly, she swept the feathers into a bag and took them to the barn and into her studio. She didn't come out for the rest of the day. Or the next. Or the next.

For a month, my mother made art from morning till night and from night till morning. I don't think she slept. I brought her food. I tried to convince her to come in and shower. Instead she stitched and stitched a story that I couldn't make out—the images were too unformed, too haphazard. She pulled the thread and knotted it tight. I couldn't make sense of anything.

"It's . . . nice, Mom," I said as I rubbed her shoulders. "I don't really know what it's about."

My mother stared at her tapestry, her mouth forming and unforming silent words, something she did a lot when she worked. "It's okay if you don't understand it," she said. "One day you will."

"Are you coming in? You need to sleep, Mom. Also—and don't take this the wrong way—but you really smell terrible. I think it's time for a shower."

She smiled. "Just a little bit longer, darling," my mother said. "There's something inside. Something that *wants to be*. But I can't find it just yet."

Four days after that conversation, we heard her cry for joy in the barn. I was making soup. Michael was sitting at the table. We looked at one another and smiled. Our mother would be coming to dinner. At last. And then she would sleep in her own bed. I set a place for her at the table and watched for the moment when she would arrive, for everything to go back to normal and for the world to be as it should.

The door opened. I held my breath.

And when my mother walked into the house, she brought that crane.

6.

The next morning, I saw my mother at breakfast, which was unusual, as she typically slept until nearly noon. She had blood seeping through the back of her T-shirt. Which was more unusual.

"What happened?" I asked.

She shrugged. "Sometimes you just get a scratch." Her eyes drifted toward the window, where they lit on the crane, stalking the grass. She smiled.

I shook my head. I looked at my mother for a long time. Her skin was pale. She needed to eat more. She clasped her hands together. She needed to wash her cuts. She needed bandages. She didn't see to any of that. Her gaze remained fixed on the window. Her face was filled with light.

Michael stomped into the kitchen. He pressed his fists into his narrow hips. "Who," he demanded, "put all those feathers in my room?"

No one had an answer.

"There are feathers *everywhere*," he fumed. My mother

didn't respond. Instead she let her hand drift toward Michael's cheek, her fingers vaguely caressing his temples and hair, while she kept her eyes focused elsewhere. Michael looked at the clock. "Are we late?" he asked.

"No," I lied. We were already quite late and were getting later by the minute. Normally, he and I rode our bikes to school—I always rode slightly behind him and with my body toward the road, so I could throw myself in front of any car that got too close. But Michael's bike had been stolen from school (most likely by a scrapper, who had taken not only the bike, but the chain and the lock and part of the bike rack as well), and mine had ceased to be operable (the gears were now more rust than metal), and so we'd have to walk. And Michael was a slow walker. Even if I dragged him behind me, he'd still be late. As for me . . . well, I wasn't sure if I'd arrive at school or not.

Michael grabbed a broom and stomped off to his room to clean it.

I turned back to my mom. There were, as far as I could tell, at least six injuries on her back. Without a word, I walked to the nearly empty cupboard by the refrigerator (also nearly empty) and grabbed the box of first-aid supplies.

"Let's see," I said, applying witch hazel to a small flannel square. My mom winced in anticipation.

"It's fine," she said.

"It's not," I said. "Remember that infection you got last year? If we can't afford insurance, we certainly can't afford another hospital visit. Have you put anything into the bank account recently?"

"It's vulgar to talk about money," my mother muttered.

"Oh, *is it*?" I demanded. "Funny, that's not what the cashier says at the store."

She turned away, avoiding my eye, and lifted the back of her shirt to let me clean her cuts. Once I got close, I realized there were bruises on the back of her neck, eight small ovals, half on each side, like fingerprints. There was also a darkening along the side of her jaw that she had covered with a bit of powder. I didn't ask about the bruises. I knew better. Sometimes, I understood without being told, when a lover was in the picture, the occasional bruise was to be expected. But the cuts were unusual. I had never seen this kind of injury on her before. She hissed as I applied the antiseptic.

"Yeah," I said. "That one's deep."

"So it goes," she said.

"I don't think it has to, Mom," I said.

She didn't reply, and instead watched the window, following the crane with her gaze. She pressed her fingers to her lips, cushioning the tips with a kiss.

I rolled my eyes. "What on earth do you see in him?" I asked.

My mother didn't look away. Her eyes remained fixed on the crane. She let her hand drift away from her face and settle on her heart.

"Everything," she said with a sigh.

7.

My mother's tapestries contained multitudes. Her method of gathering materials was as haphazard and serendipitous as the way she lived the rest of her life. She bought used clothing by the crate and unwound the threads and yarns into great piles to be strung onto the loom. Sometimes she wove in gathered marsh grasses or the gossamer puffs of pussy willows. Shoelaces. Wire from a busted lamp. Torn pieces from old quilts from the attic. Ancient coveralls from the basement. Carbon fibers from a wayward farm drone that went wild and crashed into our barn. Rusty wires and old springs from abandoned farming equipment. The skeleton of a fish, or a fox, or the remains of a wren. Each item was stitched into the story.

She had never been an early riser, my mother. I was the one who woke myself and Michael up to go to school. I was the one who made the breakfasts and packed the lunches. I was the one who figured how to stretch the food in the pantry until Mom could shop again. Mixed crumbled saltine crackers into the tuna-fish sandwiches, for example. Added extra water and salt in the canned soup. Carved the mold off the ham and hoped for the best. I was the one who watched the bank account and balanced the books. When I was very little, I was good at sums—I liked details and order and everything having its place—so my father showed me how a ledger worked and explained the basics of accounting. He showed me the tools on the computer that he used to manage my mother's sales, and the household finances, and every other finely tuned filament that created the safety net that kept us from falling to the ground. After he died, I just took over. It didn't occur to me that this was a strange task to give a nine-year-old. They were just math problems and logic puzzles, after all. I liked making everything right. And cooking dinner was no different from the projects we did in science class. I was good at school, or I was back then, and was eager to come rushing home to take over the care of my little brother so I could tell him everything I learned while my mom worked in her studio. I was good at these things, and it feels good to be good at things. Also, it just felt good to be in charge.

Despite the rumors in our little community, and despite the general belief that my mother, being an artist, was equal parts layabout and misfit and essentially a drain on the goodwill of the town, there was no one anywhere who was as hard a worker as she. Her tapestries were massive things, painstakingly layered and stitched, carefully planned, inventively sourced, and always quick to surprise. Her tapestries told stories inside of stories—the sweep of time and the tragedy of love and the persistent presence of the grave. Stories of lust and murder and birth, of rapacious hands clutching at scant resources, of trickster gods hiding in the leaves of dying trees, hoping against hope that their schemes might bear fruit before it's too late. There were appliquéd women made from feathers and barbed wire, stitched onto the backing with golden thread. Babies made from buttons. Children cut from the yellowed paper of eviction notices. Men made out of patchwork shoe leather and drenched with tears. She sewed cities composed from fibers gathered from antique seed sacks. She was a wonder, my mother. Even as a teenager, when my frustration with her reached its peak, I knew how marvelous she was.

My mother would stay up all night working on a project—sketching out a design, or spinning fiber into thread, or setting up the loom, or stitching in whatever found object she had determined must play a role in the story she sewed. Then, under the glint of the end-of-night stars, she would feed the sheep and check on her cheeses and then collapse into bed. We wouldn't see her awake until after we came home from school—and sometimes, she would still be rubbing the sleep from her eyes. Even that late in the day.

But then that crane came into our lives. And everything changed.

Within days, my mother began waking just before dawn, moving around the house scribbling notes to herself in her notebook, as the crane stalked the garden looking for snails.

"Are you sick?" I asked her, after this had been going on for more than a week. She had scratches on the backs of her arms and a wound just above her ankle. I didn't ask about them. I knew she wouldn't tell me.

"Sick? Why, no. I never get sick." She looked outside. She watched as the crane tramped across the yard. Her face seemed to shine. The crane went near the sheep, who cowered in a corner. My mother smiled. She had dark circles under her eyes. Her hair was limp.

"Sit," I said. "I'll make breakfast."

She looked at me. Her eyes were strange to me then. Hollow. Empty. The cold dark between galaxies, or the dull ache of a barren, fruitless field. Looking back on it now, I recognize those eyes. I've seen those same eyes on different women in the years since—my girlfriends, my roommates, my coworkers. I saw them on a neighbor once, before I called the cops on her husband. I myself have had those eyes. But only once. She blinked. The hollowness remained. I shivered. I didn't know what I was seeing.

"How can I eat," she asked me, "when I am so full of love?"

I ignored this and made her a bowl of scrambled eggs anyway. I kissed the top of her head as I served her, as though I was the mother and she was the child. She didn't eat a single bite. I ended up giving it to Michael, who ate it cold.

That night, I dreamed almost entirely of feathers. Feathers on the ground. Feathers in my hair. Feathers in my mouth. I called for Michael, but only feathers came out. I rubbed my eyes, but they too were made of feathers. Beginning to panic, I ran outside to the barn and climbed up to my mother's studio in the loft. There, I saw the crane standing at my mother's loom, sewing my mother's face into a tapestry.

No, it was just an image of my mother's face.

I stared harder. Time stopped.

No, it was her actual face, the skin stretched thin and garishly wide, the edges still bloody. My mother's eyes blinked.

I shook my head. Dream logic collided with actual logic, clouding the scene. I squinted. The face of my mother in the tapestry smiled serenely. "Don't worry, my love," she said to me. "It doesn't hurt at all. And you haven't stopped to admire Father's cape."

Don't look at the crane's cape, I told myself. I didn't know why. I woke with a gasp, drenched and shaking.

The next day, after school, I decided to check in on my mother at her studio. Before the crane, my mother always welcomed us to sit with her while she worked. Mostly we just read books and enjoyed being near her even though she ignored us. When she made art, Mom was focused and still. She had none of the fleshy, physical ease in the world that defined her the rest of the time. Her movements were tight and controlled, her breathing shallow and even, and she never deviated her focus away from her stitches and threads, her drawings and plans, the fragile mechanisms of her giant loom. For a long time, I had very little concept of my mom's job at all—her time at her loom and at her desk were both just a thing she did, something that snatched her attention and imprisoned it for hours. Michael and I preferred her when she was Mom the mother rather than Mom the artist.

Still, even if she wasn't much of a talker when she worked, we knew we were always *welcome*. She always made a space for us. She was always happy to have us there. Always.

Which was why it was so surprising to find the door to the studio locked.

"Mom?" I called from outside.

She didn't answer.

I cupped my hands around my mouth. *"Mom?"* I said louder.

Still nothing. I could hear my mother and the crane inside. The crane squawking and murmuring in an annoyed sort of way. My mother's voice smooth and soothing.

"I know, darling," I heard her say reassuringly. "We're almost there. I'll make everything beautiful."

I had no way of knowing what she meant.

8.

Shortly before my dad died, he and I spent the day in his sickroom, curled up in our nest of quilts, each made by my mother and each a riot of color and figures and motion. My father's favorite quilt was usually draped on top, his hands drifting over its bright colors and outlandish story-telling—in addition to depictions of beautiful witches and petulant giants and entire cities populated by birds, at the very center, my mother had affixed a man and a woman on their wedding day, their hands clasped and their faces nearly touching. Each had red embroidery thread stitched where their hearts should be, connected to one another by a series of knots. The man was faded and vague—the only figure in the quilt that was gray instead of multicolored. The woman had a pair of iridescent wings and feet made of feathers. She had a button fastened over her mouth.

I cuddled close to my father. The smell of him had been getting more pungent by the day, a smell that I would learn much later was reminiscent of the ocean as it ebbs away—decomposition and dissolution and salt. I had never seen the ocean and imagined that it must be something like a cornfield—a whir, a whisper, and a wave, stretching to the edge of the sky. He winced a lot in those days. And sometimes he shook. He had tubes that notched into his nose to help him breathe, and a tube going straight into his arm, dripping a clear liquid, and another that sometimes attached to a port on his chest.

I could spend all day with my dad, and often did. We would read books together or I would draw and he would praise my efforts. He taught me how to do math games and logic puzzles and the trick of adding or multiplying impressively large numbers in an impressively short amount of time. ("It's just patterns, you see? Once you can see the patterns a number makes, once you can recognize the trick of it, then simple arithmetic becomes indistinguishable from complex summations. Your brain knows it before your eye even has time to process the whole thing.") He taught me how to identify birds from their calls and how to catch a fly between my finger and my thumb. He even taught me how to pick a lock, with a box of tools that he kept hidden under the bed because he knew my mother would never approve. Later, I moved that box into my closet without telling anyone. It was the first time I learned that sometimes it was best to keep what I could do to myself.

My dad kept his hands on my hair or shoulders or curled around my own hands to keep his trembling away. My mom was in her studio, Michael either in a sling or tied to her back. She worked all the time, back then. Sometimes she didn't want to come to bed at night. Sometimes she didn't come into the house at all. I would see my dad's gaze drift to the window. I could feel his rattling sigh.

I noticed him looking and I frowned.

He noticed my frowning and admonished me.

"What's with the face?" my father said.

I didn't know what to say. I wanted my mother to be here with us, nestled in the bed. And Michael, too. The fact that she wasn't irked me deeply—an uncomfortable *wrongness* that itched and pulled, like a sweater that didn't fit. I didn't quite know why. We were supposed to be together. And the fact that we weren't was Mom's fault, I was pretty sure.

I didn't have words for any of this, but Dad wanted an answer. I pouted for a moment. "Mom's boring," I said, finally. It wasn't exactly what I felt, but it was the closest sentence I could think of that aimed at the truth.

Dad took this information in, his face grave. He was the only adult I knew who ever took me seriously. "I see," he said. He coughed into a tissue, deftly whisking it into a pocket before I could look at it. "I never thought of her that way, but of course you know more than I do about such things."

"I do," I agreed.

"Did you know," he said, changing the subject, "that in old stories, weavers were often considered to be magical."

"What's a weaver?" I asked.

"Mommy's a weaver," he said. "That's her job."

I frowned. "I thought she drew pictures and then made stuff with string."

"Right," my father said, his hand on my cheek. His hands were so gentle then. "Same thing."

"I think I already knew that," I said, because I wanted my father to think I was smart.

"Indeed," he said, using his serious voice. It thrilled me to my core to be taken seriously. "Well," my father continued, "if you want to get specific about it, Mommy's a weaver and then some. A fancy weaver. An *artist* weaver." Another shuddering breath. "There are lots of stories about weavers, you know. Ancient, powerful stories. The Greeks, for example, told stories of the Fates. They were mean old ladies who stitched calamities and sorrows into the fabric of people's lives. One pull of the thread and love could be lost, or a life could end, or a kingdom could land in ruins."

He coughed again. Talking sometimes took a lot out of him. I handed him his water. He had a hard time swallowing, and some of the water dribbled down his chin. He cleared his throat.

"In Ireland," he continued, "the goddess Brigantia sat at her loom and wove the whole land into being, stitch by beautiful stitch. And broken stitch." Another cough. "In China, the goddess Zhinü stitched each of the stars into the heavens, and wove the silver river streaking across the sky. In ancient Egypt, the goddess Neith wove two kingdoms together, and the Vikings sang sagas about the valkyries who wove on looms fitted with severed heads for weights and used arrows to pull the thread from end to terrible end. Weavers could tell your fortune or remove enchantments or change your fate. You could weave a happy marriage, a healthy family, a doomed generation, an unraveling birthright. You never want to make a weaver angry, I'll tell you that much."

He coughed again. And shook. He pushed a button connected to the tube in his arm. He would be sleeping soon.

I brought my hands to his face and peered into his eyes, wanting to be present for the moment when his consciousness blinked out.

"Is Mommy magic?" I asked. My voice was serious. I didn't believe it for a second—why would she be magic? Clearly, I would have known by now if she was. Still. I wanted to be sure.

Dad's eyelids grew heavy. They opened and closed slowly, like ocean waves. He didn't answer right away.

After a moment, "There's one story about an old man who rescues a crane. The crane falls in love with the man, and so she turns herself into a woman who weaves the most beautiful fabric that anyone's ever seen. This he sells, and becomes prosperous. He can hardly believe his good fortune. A beautiful wife. A successful business. And they're happy in their marriage. In their lives together. They're so, so happy. For a little while. But then he gets greedy. Because men get greedy. Oh, he is grateful at first. But then he wants more and more from her. He takes and takes and takes. After a while, he only sees what she *doesn't* make, what she *hasn't* achieved. He becomes obsessed with the fortune that her future handiwork has *not yet* earned. She forgives him this greed, and continues her work, constantly making more and more for the man she loves. She only asks him to leave her be while she works. Her only rule is that he must not open the door to the room where her loom sits, that he must not disturb her. Only then can they both be happy. But one day he can't stand it. She's too slow, he thinks. She's not as wonderful as he wants her to be. Sales are down. He wants to be richer, and more important. She's not enough for him, and, he realizes, *she can never be enough.* All that beauty, all that art, and yet he feels that she has failed. That she has failed *him*. He bursts through the door to admonish her, raising his voice. But instead of his beautiful wife at the loom, he sees a beautiful crane, weaving and weaving and weaving. The crane stops her work, and shakes her head. She turns to the window, hops to the sill, and flies away. And she never returns."

His pupils went wide. He sighed with his mouth open. He was quiet for a long moment.

"Is Mommy magic?" I asked again.

"I never liked that story." His voice was very slow. "I certainly would never be that guy. I can't imagine refusing a single request your mother makes. Besides. Why is it a crane? Cranes are mean. Cruel, you know? Just ask any frog or fish in the pond. A crane is a predator just like any other predator—sneaky, and opportunistic. Not one of them would have the patience for weaving, or for beauty for its own sake. A crane would make someone else do it for him. A mouse maybe. Or a beautiful spider. He'd work it nearly to death, and then he'd eat it."

His eyelids became heavy, settling deep in their grooves. His hands drifted away.

I settled in close, keeping my eyes on the window to my mother's studio across the yard. Sometimes I would see my mother's silhouette against the far wall. Sometimes I would see glimpses of whatever tapestry she was weaving, when she readjusted the light.

I frowned. It didn't look magic at all.

9.

Almost a month after the crane arrived, a social worker stopped by the house.

It wasn't a surprise. Or, at least, I wasn't surprised. I had ditched at least one class—sometimes all of them—every single week since school began. Honestly, the only surprise was that it took this long. It was the end of March, after all.

The social worker wore beige. Beige shoes. Beige slacks. A smart beige jacket. A creamy silk blouse, open at her throat. A silver pendant in the shape of a bird hung from a chain around her neck. Her dark curls had been assembled into a tight mound on the top of her head with a braid wound around the base. She had eyeglasses that came to upturned points at the sides, where two little green lights blinked like emeralds, indicating that they were connected wirelessly to the tablet that rested in her open portfolio.

"I'm required to inform you that I'm recording this interaction," she said cheerfully. She had small teeth and red lips. She flashed a grin.

"Yeah," I said. I pressed my lips into a tight line in case she missed the disdain in my voice. "We can already see that." I gestured to the image of me and a frightened-looking Michael staring out of the tablet's smudged screen. I waved at myself waving back.

"I suppose you can," she said. "Your file informs me that you're a clever girl. But not so clever as to make it to school every day."

"I always make it to school," I said.

"Of course you do. We have a video compilation in the office of you flipping off the front-door camera. Every day. One might think it would get old. Actually, I meant to say that you're not so clever as to *stay* in school every day. Clever girls stay in school so they can go to college, which gives them wings to fly far, far away when they're grown. The sky's the limit, as they say. Isn't that what you want? Your teachers tell me that you're a bright spark with a brighter future, and yet it seems you care so very little about your education. I'm curious to find out why." She flashed another grin. "I'm a curious lady, you see."

She stood on the porch. I stood in the door. I had not yet invited her in. I wasn't sure I would. She wasn't allowed to just walk across the threshold without expressed verbal consent. There were rules to this sort of thing. Even I knew that.

"I mean," I said flatly. I didn't roll my eyes because it would have been too obvious a cliché. But I wanted to. "Calling anything that happens in that school an 'education'"—I used air quotes—"is a bit of a stretch." Her cheerfulness flickered, just a bit. "Last week my history teacher showed us a filmstrip. An actual filmstrip. I had no idea those things still existed. It had to have been a hundred years old."

The social worker pursed her lips. "That does sound historical. Maybe you should have paid attention."

"My teacher didn't. He fell asleep in the middle." I pulled my sweater around my shoulders more tightly and crossed my arms. Michael, standing close, began to shiver. It was chilly out, and I was letting out the heat. We couldn't stand in the doorway all day. "And anyway, the filmstrip wasn't even on topic. The whole business is a waste of time."

None of this was true, by the way. My teachers were fine. Just boring. Irrelevant in ways that I couldn't exactly articulate but irked me all the same. I didn't much care for high school—the pageantry of it, the performative bravado, the unwritten rules, the crush of people with their faces and smells. I didn't much care for the kids who looked at me askance and wondered—or asked, out loud and to my face—how much I was like my mom. Was I artistic like her? Was I slutty like her? Was I vaguely tragic in a whispered town lore sort of way? (I was nothing like my mother. I was everything like my mother. Both at the same time.) All I really wanted to do was find a quiet place where I could draw and stare at the sky and have my own thoughts. Sometimes, I'd join up with other kids skipping class—stoner kids, mostly. Or drinkers. I didn't much care for either of those things, but we found other things to do to pass the time. I stuck with any particular group until inevitably one person would ask a question about my mom that began with "Is it true that," at which point I'd bounce. I don't remember any of their names. I'm not sure I ever learned them in the first place.

The social worker looked me up and down. She peered at Michael, who hid behind my legs. My mother was in the studio. Making art. Making eyes at the crane. And other things that I did not want to even think about. Hopefully it was just the art.

"Is your mother home?" the social worker asked.

"No," I said.

"Can I come in?"

I deflated a bit. If I said no, she'd be back. With legal papers asserting her right to look at whatever she wanted. And she'd be on a mission. I quickly made an inventory in my head of the total contents inside the cupboards and the refrigerator. A package of hot dogs that had developed a bit of a slime, but a quick rinse would make them good as new. A few apples with wrinkly skins that I could either slice or peel. And a precious round of one of my mother's cheeses. Mostly she sold those for money to keep the lights on, but every once in a while, as a treat, she kept one for us. I sliced it thin to make it last and didn't much treasure the thought of sharing it with this stranger.

"Of course," I said, stepping back and sweeping my arm open in a grand gesture to welcome her in, my face settling on a subtle smirk that I hoped she would notice. "Welcome to our humble home. Please make yourself comfortable. Are you hungry? Or can I get you something to drink?"

"What lovely manners," she said, walking past me into the house, her gaze swiveling this way and that. I knew she was scanning with her glasses, making a recording. She took a sweeping look around the room, going up and down, pausing briefly at the wall hangings my mother had made (some nudity, but not enough to raise alarms) and the tapestry experiments that had become throw blankets. I silently congratulated myself for giving the place a good scrub the day before and sweeping again when I got home. You'd never even guess that a crane was staying here. There wasn't a feather anywhere. I did notice her eyes resting pointedly on a pair of my father's shoes that the crane had abandoned, with wide holes to accommodate his talons. She shook her head. They didn't look usable, after all. She didn't have to worry about who they belonged to.

"Well, I was well brought up," I said more sniffily than I intended. "I could make us a plate of cheese and crackers if you'd like." This wasn't true either. We had no crackers. Hopefully she wouldn't notice.

She smiled at that. A genuine smile. "I've had your mother's cheese, and as delicious as that sounds, I think I'll pass. I'm not particularly hungry. How about just a glass of water."

We sat at the kitchen table, the three of us. She let her eyes rest on every corner. The photographs on the wall. The books on the shelves. The mostly bare pantry. No guns visible, though we did own one—my grandfather's old shotgun. We kept it in the storage room in the basement, locked in its box and tucked into an oilcloth to keep out the dust and bugs and damp. Every year, I took it out to clean it, just like my dad taught me, and check the box of ammunition to look for signs of any degrading. My father had taught me to shoot when I was quite little. Before he was confined to his bed. He showed me how to hold a target in one eye and focus intently. He taught me how to stay still and keep my breath steady and slow. How to pull gently on the trigger—so soft that it wouldn't even know it was being pulled. Later, in the months after my father died, my mom made me practice for hours—targets, tin cans, a sand-filled sack thrown into the air. I was pretty good. A natural shot, Mom said. She told me that it was an important skill to keep up, because you never did know.

But that was a long time ago. Neither of us had touched it in years.

Michael said nothing. He rattled the ice in his glass. He slurped his water. He stared at the social worker with wide eyes. I put my arm around him and gave him a squeeze, letting him know that I'd take care of it. I always took care of it.

She made small talk for a while. She asked me for my thoughts on the new principal (I had none) and my interest in perhaps volunteering to do set design for the school play (also none). She asked about my mom's work, about the clients who would sometimes come and go, about the man who coordinates her online sales and handles her contracts and payments. "Bruce, his name is, is that right? Funny how I've never run into him around town. Does he . . . spend a lot of time here? With you. Or with your brother."

"Well," I said carefully, "I wouldn't say so. Bruce really keeps to himself. And these days, a person can really work from anywhere. Doesn't have to be here in town, when it comes down to it. Bruce can go where he pleases. I don't see him much. As far as I can tell, he just lives in the computer and on the phone." I reached under the table and squeezed Michael's hand. He knew, of course, that Bruce was made up. I was Bruce. I was the one who handled my mother's sales. I was the one who reached out to potential buyers. I was the one who wrote the newsletter and kept the website up to date. I was the one who fed our accounts and minded our bills and paid our debts and made sure the lights stayed on. But people were more likely to take me seriously when they thought the person emailing or texting them was some guy named Bruce. I even had a program on my phone to change my voice, for the rare occasions where I had to talk to someone on the phone.

I caught Michael's eye and winked.

"So," the social worker said, pressing her palms together and bringing her fingertips to her lips, "Bruce isn't someone I have to worry about. Are you *safe* at home, is what I'm asking." She paused. Her face became soft and serious. She laid her hands on the table, palms up. "Honestly, I mean. Safety is my main concern, and it is why I'm here today. Are you *safe*? Is Michael safe? Is this home a safe place for you?"

I thought about my mother with the cuts on her back. The bruises on her neck. I thought about the crane and his swagger and leer. I thought about the dream about the fish and the sharp tip of that cruel beak. And I thought about the feathers in Michael's room. The irrational terror of our sheep. I tried to make my face expressionless. Just like my mom.

"Safe as houses," I said.

She gave me a card with a number for my mom to call, and a pamphlet on the importance of staying in school, and another one about birth control, just in case. And a third earnestly explaining why drugs are bad and that I should not use them. She told me that she was surprised that the truancy officer hadn't been by. She told me that she would chew him out on my behalf and send him down so we could make a plan to get me back on track. Whatever that meant. She told me to call her whenever I wanted.

"Everyone deserves someone looking out for her," she said, doing one more scan around the room, saving every detail of our house into her tablet. "You call me the second anything doesn't feel right. Even if you can't put your finger on *why* it doesn't feel right. When kids skip school, they're running away from *something*. And that something is rarely school."

"Oh really," I said more scathingly than I intended. "What, then, do you think they're running from? Do you honestly think I'm running away from something?"

The social worker took off her glasses and slid them into her pocket. No more recording. It was, for a moment, just the two of us. Even Michael seemed to vanish a bit. I swallowed. She looked me full in the face, her eyes suddenly gentle and wide open. Like she was seeing me for the first time. Like she, too, wanted to be *seen*. "I don't think either of us needs to answer that question. The answer is fairly obvious, don't you think?" I didn't know why, but her words hit me hard—a deep, startling blow. She put her hand, briefly, on my shoulder. I was pretty sure that wasn't allowed, but I appreciated it anyway. "What I do know is this: once a person starts to run, it's really hard for them to stop." Her eyes slid to my brother, who stared up at her with a stricken expression. "And sometimes they never do. And that's a real shame." She put her glasses back on. Her face once again became terse and businesslike. "I'll be back soon. Be good until then. I'll see myself out."

Michael held my hand as she walked out of the house. He squeezed my fingers very tightly.

"I don't want you to go away," he said, his voice already starting to shake. "You're not really going to run, are you?"

I looked out at the drones hovering over the field, moving back and forth, scanning the land with their electric eyes. The electric fence hummed, hemming us in.

"Buddy," I said, "where would I even go?"

10.

Having a crane living in the house presents a certain set of problems. First, there is the issue of his gait, which due to his larger-than-most-cranes size meant that I had to predict the exceptionally wide potential swing of his body in order to protect objects on tables and shelves from being knocked off.

For example, in his first week, he took a wide step, swung far to the left, and his tail feathers knocked down one of the only framed photos that we had of our whole family before Dad died—with Mom holding Michael in the crook of her arm and me sitting on Dad's knee with my hand curled around his shrunken face. The glass shattered and scratched a groove along my dad's right cheek.

"What did you *do*?" I yelled at the crane, my eyes blurry with tears. I picked up the glass and instantly cut my fingers. I wanted to throw a handful right into his face. Mom stood between us, her arm out in an accusatory point.

Toward *me*. The *gall of it*.

"How dare you!" my mother shouted. "We don't care about *things* in this family. What's a *thing*? What's the point of a *thing*? It doesn't live or breathe or love. The only value we must keep close to our hearts is the *living*. Inanimate objects are only tomorrow's trash."

I gasped and turned my face away so I didn't have to look at her. I carried the glass in one hand and carefully picked up the picture with the other, taking care not to splotch it with blood.

"Mom," I said acidly, "you're an *artist*. You make *things* for a living." I gestured at a mini-tapestry that hung directly behind her on the far wall. But she didn't listen and she didn't even seem to register that I was speaking at all. Instead she turned to the crane. Her hands in his feathers. Her face caressing his face.

"I'm sorry, my love," she soothed. "She's just a child and she can't possibly understand. But she will." She turned toward me, her face altered slightly. It was a look I did not recognize. "She'll see soon enough."

I had no intention of seeing anything of the kind.

The other consideration concerned the crane's diet. On his first evening in the house, when I served him the soup, he wouldn't touch it. He moved the leaves of the salad around a bit, hunting around for something—bugs, I figured out later. And then fell into a grumpy slump. It wasn't until the following evening, when he saw a mouse tear across the kitchen floor, that it became apparent to me that his dietary needs were different from those of the rest of us. The mouse scampered, and in a flash, the crane pendulumed forward from the fulcrum of his hip joint, the spear of his beak landing on the creature with astonishing speed and force. The mouse popped like a balloon. In the same smooth motion, the crane threw it in the air and caught it in his throat, swallowing it in one gulp.

We were silent for a moment. Then Michael threw up right into his bowl. Then he ran into his room to cry. He loved mice. He loved all small creatures.

I pointed at the bloody splotch on the carpet. "Is anyone going to clean that up?"

My mother didn't say anything. The crane went outside to hunt. My mother smiled indulgently. "Someone's still hungry," she said, and sighed.

Right away, I worried about Michael's pet hamsters, Goldilocks and Kublai Khan, who lived in a small cage by the window in the storage room.

They were both gone by the end of the month.

11.

Eight weeks after the crane's arrival, it remained a fixture in our house. I went downstairs for breakfast that morning, hoping once again to find him gone, and once again I was disappointed. Michael sat at one side of the table, staring at his empty cereal bowl in silence, while my mother sat on the other side, canoodling with the crane. She had cuts on her neck. Cuts on her breasts. Cuts up and down her arms. Some so deep that she had neatly stitched them shut. I had expressed alarm—often and loudly—but she waved my concerns away.

"Paper cuts," she said. "And I've been meaning to fix that damn loom. Occupational hazard." The crane slapped her ass with the underside of his foot, scoring the fabric with his sharp talon. It hooked the pocket of her jeans and yanked her back into his lap, ripping the seam just a bit. She fell into his body—both soft feathers and hard angles—with a laugh. "Has there ever been a happier couple?" she said.

The crane squawked.

I caught Michael's eye and pretended to barf. Michael, stony faced, did not show that he noticed. He didn't speak all morning.

Michael and I walked slowly to school that day. We were running late again. I didn't really care. I was failing my English class. We were already on the dark side of second semester, so my prospects of turning that grade around were fairly nonexistent. There's not much difference, I felt, between a high F and a low F. There wasn't much sense in hurrying. It was April, and too hot for April. The morning sun beat our faces hard, as we walked down that long, black road.

Finally, Michael stopped in his tracks. He turned to me, crinkling his eyebrows together. "I don't like Father," he muttered with a frown, his gaze tilted towards my shoes.

"Don't call him Father," I said. We didn't even call our own father Father. We called him Dad. Not that Michael remembered this. He was only a baby, after all. *Daddy's little miracle,* my father called him, since the doctors had told him that his radiation and chemotherapy had long ago rendered him sterile. *Yes,* I remember my mother saying vaguely, her eyes drifting out the window. *A miracle.*

"She didn't go to the farmers market on Saturday," Michael said. I already knew about this. And I was worried, too. It had been a while since she had sold one of her pieces, and we definitely needed the money. But Michael was only six. He should be worrying about learning how to tie his shoes, not about our mother's checking account. I did my best to soothe him.

"Sometimes grown-ups don't always do what you'd expect," I said, hoping that it sounded reasonable and authoritative enough to put an end to the topic. But Michael wasn't done.

"She *always* goes to the farmers market." He was a serious boy. Prone to tears. I noticed that the slick at the rim of his eyelids was deepening. He had a mop of brown curls that I should have combed that morning, but I didn't. He was likely to start sobbing soon, and then I'd have a mess dropping him off at school.

"She *mostly* goes to the farmers market. Sometimes she doesn't."

He would not be dissuaded. "She *always* goes. And so do I. And I help sell the cheese. And I don't always like selling the cheese, but I like sitting with Mom. And then she takes the money and buys groceries. She didn't buy groceries this Saturday. I had to eat peanut butter with no bread for breakfast. My mouth is very sticky now."

This was true. And so was mine.

And Michael didn't even know the whole story. There are tasks to the making of cheese that have to be done in a certain order and in a certain way—even as the cheese ages. The rounds hadn't been turned, for example. I had to do it, and I might have been too late. The humidity needed to be checked three times a day and adjusted as needed, and I was fairly certain my mother wasn't doing any of that. I didn't know how many rounds would make it through the season, much less age long enough to be sold. The new batch of hastily pressed wheels sat untouched in the corner of the barn, souring as we spoke, and would probably have to be thrown away. And the freezer truck had come just the day before, and my mother sent the delivery back. All of a sudden, my mother couldn't be bothered with cheese. The only thing that mattered to her now was whatever she was doing in her studio with that crane. And whatever *that* was, continually left her bloody and sighing and syrupy sweet. It was vile. I did my best to shove these thoughts away so that Michael wouldn't see them writing themselves on my face.

"Is Mom okay?" Michael asked, wiping his nose with the back of his hand.

I put my arm around his shoulder and gave him a squeeze. "Don't worry, buddy," I said. "She's fine."

This was a lie, obviously.

My mother wasn't fine.

12.

Sometimes, realizations occur in fits and starts. A moment of clarity here. A loud *aha* there. A slap on the forehead at the something so glaringly obvious that a child could have figured it out.

My first realization was this: that a man, an actual man, was living in our house as well. In addition to the crane. I heard his footsteps in the hall at night, pacing back and forth after my mother went to sleep. I could smell the stink of him from under my door. I started keeping my desk chair braced under the doorknob when I went to sleep, just in case. From my mother's locked bedroom, I could hear the crane's squawk, and then a man's lisping rumble, and then my mother's sigh. Once I heard something that sounded distinctly like a fist hitting a face. The next day my mother had a bruise under her eye. Another on her shoulder. She tried to cover each with foundation, but I saw them all the same.

Doorjamb, she evaded. *The sheep headbutt me sometimes,* she lied.

"Who *else* is here?" I asked one morning, noticing that the jug of milk that was halfway full the night before was now empty, and the last four slices of bologna had vanished, as had the entire package of prewrapped cheese slices. We typically bought groceries every Saturday—the whole list when we were flush, just the essentials when we were tight, and then whatever happened to be on sale and under budget on the weeks when we scraped the bottom of the barrel. We had been at the bottom of the barrel for so long I couldn't even remember what flush looked like.

My mother shrugged. "Sometimes people get peckish."

"You're not answering the question. I know you didn't eat this food. And I know I didn't. Michael went to bed early. Who drank the milk? Who ate the meat and cheese? I was counting on that today, Mom. That . . . *thing*—"

"Hey," Mom said, her eyes flashing. I ignored it.

"—only eats bugs and fish and stuff. Mom. *Who else is here?"*

My mother gently traced her curls out of her eyes with the backs of her fingers. "I'm not sure what you're talking about," she said. "This house contains you, your brother, Father, and myself. There's no one else."

"He's not my father," I said, crossing my arms.

"We'll see," my mother said.

"But what about—" I began, but my mother had a thought. She pulled out her notebook and began scribbling, her mouth folded over itself and her eyes vague. I knew there was no talking to her when she got like this.

"Darling," she said, not to me, but to the crane. He was

nowhere to be seen. *"Darling,"* she said louder. The crane squawked from outside. "I . . . I think I might have it." And she snapped her notebook shut and hurried out of the house. They disappeared into the studio without another word, locking the doors behind them. I went outside, baffled, and stared at the space that no longer contained either of them. My mother. The crane. Even when they vanished, their presence remained, like the shadow of a stain after months of washing. The sheep complained in their pens. They needed to be fed. They missed my mother.

"Give me a second," I said, trying to sound soothing, though I know for a fact that I wasn't. My mother was the soother of the family, not me. The sheep bellowed back.

I grabbed a sack of feed from the shed and grabbed the hose to fill up their water trough. The sheep pressed together in the corner of their enclosure. They were agitated and jumpy. And muddy, I noticed suddenly. It had rained the night before, but it didn't really explain where all of the caked-in mud came from. I showed them my hands and let them smell me. One sheep trembled.

"Hey Nix," I said, trying to quiet them down. "Hey Beverly. Hey Jean." The sheep would not be calmed. There was a pile of feathers in the pen. The sheep avoided it. I filled their food bin and hopped the fence to look more closely at the feathers. The sheep bellowed, as though warning me away. I bent down. They definitely looked like crane feathers. The crane never seemed interested in the sheep before. And why would he climb in there just to molt? I looked closer.

"BAAAA," implored Beverly.

I moved the feathers away and the sheep relaxed.

Mostly. I looked closer. There, in the hardened mud, were two footprints. Man sized.

"Baa," said Nix, pressing her head to my hands, demanding scratches and strokes. She needed comfort. Nix was by far the neediest of the sheep. She used her body to herd me away from the footprints, as though they were toxic somehow. Poisonous.

"I'm inclined to agree," I murmured.

13.

Whatever my mom thought she found when she rushed to the studio that day turned out to be a bust. They both returned to the house that night under a cloud, their frustration with one another spilling out into the space around them. My mother's words became tight and waspish. The crane's movements became abrupt and vaguely violent. They were both all hard edges and sharp points. For a brief time, the canoodling thankfully stopped. I hoped, wildly, that this would mean that the crane would migrate at last and we would be rid of him, but no such luck.

The crane stayed.

Their bad mood with one another lingered for about a week, but in time my mother softened and cajoled the crane to soften in turn. There was nothing soft about the crane, but certainly their nightly enthusiastic yawps in the bedroom slowly returned, much to my annoyance.

"When is he going to leave?" Michael asked me one morning at breakfast. He had been asking and asking. At first I said, "Soon." But now there was nothing to do but shrug.

The truancy officer called five times over the course of that week. Since my mom never bothered locking her phone, and largely left it sitting randomly around the house, I was able to find these messages and erase them. I don't think it mattered in any case. My mother wasn't much interested in my education at that point. And she wasn't interested in having any sort of conversation with anyone who wasn't the crane.

She thought only about the crane.

And the art she made with the crane.

The art that we weren't allowed to see.

The wrongness of the situation rested heavily on my shoulders. It looped around my belly and chest, winding tighter and tighter until I could barely breathe.

On the following Tuesday, the lights went out again, but it was too late to call the electric company, so Michael and I made dinner in the dark.

The refrigerator was empty, other than for an almost depleted bottle of mustard and a large jar of sweet pickle relish. There were also a couple of elderly carrots that had essentially transformed into ropes. I used all of this and decided to consider it a blessing that nothing would spoil overnight. I hunted through the pantry to find something to feed my brother and me. And my mother. If she ate. Which was doubtful.

My mother didn't come in for dinner when I called her. She had been in the studio all day. With that crane. She didn't go for her usual walks. She didn't sit in her swing chair under the oak tree to look out on the fields. She didn't see to the sheep (I had to do that) or sweep the house (also me). She didn't hug Michael when he got home, or swing him around, or tell him he was her bestest boy. I offered to do it instead, but he told me it wasn't the same.

"Are you ready to eat?" I asked Michael. He set the table with place mats he found.

We sat in the plastic chairs next to the back stoop, Michael and I. We watched the door, waiting for my mother to emerge. Candlelight flickered in the windows.

We waited for a long, long time.

The sun had set, but the night was still quite warm. I heard my mother laugh in the barn. I heard another sound— the crane keening loud and low. He sounded more like a man every day.

Or maybe something else. There was a story about that. My father used to tell it to me.

"We're so close, baby," I heard my mom say more than once. "We're nearly there."

Michael's stomach rumbled. We couldn't wait any longer. I brought our dinner out to the chairs. Michael and I ate bowls of baked beans and canned ham topped with relish and mostly stale saltine crackers for dinner. We washed it down with Kool-Aid made from packets that were so old they had hardened into lumps. There was no sugar, so we drank it tart. Our sheep bellowed in their pen. I had already fed them, but they didn't care. They missed my mother. We all missed my mother. Michael and the sheep and I had all become accustomed to pinning our eyes on the old barn door, waiting for her to emerge.

Finally, after it was nearly dark, she and the crane walked out into the yard. She leaned against him, her upper body partially draped over his wings, her neck resting on his neck.

She was so thin. Her jeans hung on her jutted hip bones. Her step was light and fragile, like a bird's.

Without warning, the crane disentangled himself, shrugged her off, and began to hunt for crickets and frogs in the weeds. My mother continued unsteadily across the yard, but halfway between the barn and the kitchen door, she missed a step and fell to the ground in a deep swoon.

"Mom!" I yelled, bursting out of the kitchen door at a run. The crane couldn't be bothered. He continued to peck through the tangles at the edge of the yard. The only thing that seemed to unnerve him was the sound of the drones over the fields on the other side of the fence. Every time they got close, he puffed out his feathers and squawked. His wing had healed by that time, mostly. When he extended his full wingspan, one side drooped slightly. That didn't make it any less impressive.

My mom had already pulled herself to her knees when I got to her. She rubbed her face and shook her head.

"Don't worry about me, darling," she said vaguely. "I honestly don't know what's gotten into me these days." She curled and uncurled her spine, like a cat. Her fingers were scabbed in some places, the skin glued shut in others. Blood seeped from an open wound on her palm. She had abrasions on her arms, cuts on her shoulders. She stretched to the side, and I saw a gash above her left hip that she had stitched neatly closed, using pink thread. She had dark circles under her eyes. She put her hands limply on my shoulders as she readied herself to hoist her way up. It took several tries.

"I can tell you exactly what's gotten into you," I said, shooting a poisonous look at the crane.

"Enough," she said, wobbling to her feet. I curled my

arm around her waist and held it there. She was so light I thought she might blow away. "What would your father say if he heard you talking like that?"

"He's not my father."

"We'll see," my mother said, a sleepy and indulgent smile playing on her lips. Her legs gave way for a moment. She hung on to me the way a vine clings to an oak tree. She was as weightless as dry leaves.

"Mom," I said flatly, "you need to eat food."

"You silly girl," she said with a soft smile. "I have—"

"Love is not enough, Mom," I said with a flat finality. "You're injured. And you're weak from hunger. Please eat food." She wobbled as she walked. She turned her face away from me. "And also go to the grocery store, Mom. This can't go on. Our cupboards are nearly empty. Michael is only six, and he needs to eat. A spoonful of peanut butter is not an appropriate breakfast for a little boy."

That seemed to shake her out of her stupor. Her body tensed. The look she gave me was sharp and searching. "My baby's hungry?" she said, her voice suddenly both vigilant and desperate, in equal measures.

I considered how to answer this. "Well, not right this second," I said. "He ate a really substandard supper, but it *was* food, and he's full. He's fine for now. But he will be hungry soon, Mom. You have to go to the store. Or first go to the bank and then the store. You haven't been selling *anything*, and we can't live on . . ." I glared at the crane. "Whatever that fool thinks he can provide. You can't live on love, Mom. It's not possible."

"Don't be rude," my mother said.

"I'm *honest*," I retorted more harshly than I intended. If my mother had feathers, she would have puffed them out. I tried to relax my tone. "Listen," I said. "There's some kind of fancy gathering happening right now over at one of the inns. I forget which one. There's slick cars everywhere and tourists snapping pictures of literally the dumbest things. Maybe I should see if anyone's been asking after your work. Or I can follow up with the people who responded to the newsletter. Maybe someone wants to see what you've been working on up in the studio. You know. The new project. If you're too busy, I could be the one to arrange—"

My mother squawked, like a bird, and smacked my hands away. *"It's not for you,"* she hissed. She traced her gaze back toward the barn. "And don't be crass. Not everything is for *sale*," she said with distaste. "Art, true art, exists only to transform. And it is only truly art when it *does* transform. The maker. The viewer. Everyone. The transactional nature of what you are suggesting makes me *sick*." She looked back out onto the crane. And past the crane. Out onto the wide-open fields and the wider sky. She sighed a bit.

"Mom," I said. I pressed my knuckles to my mouth for a moment, trying to keep myself from saying something I might regret. "The transactional nature of what I'm suggesting is literally how you've made a living for my whole life." I stared at her. Her face was blank. Did she really not understand? "You're an artist, Mom. You make art. You *sell* art. For your job. People buy art. They've always bought art. Since, whenever. The Romans or something. What has gotten into you anyway?"

She pursed her lips primly. "There are some things," my mother said, "that money simply cannot buy."

This was obviously insane, so I decided to ignore it. I helped my mother inside and sat her at the table, setting a bowl of baked beans and shredded ham and relish and crackers in front of her. My mother stared at the food as though she had never seen such a thing in her entire life.

"Eat, Mom," I said. Michael sat on her lap. He tried to feed her with a spoon, as though she were a baby. She smiled and pretended to lap it up, but I saw her spit it into a napkin. Michael must have noticed this as well, because he stopped trying.

My mother's eyes drifted to an ancient photograph on the wall. Three couples, all in a line and all dressed for a shared wedding day. She smiled ruefully, running the corner of the uneaten cracker from her lip to her cheek. She held it between two fingers, like a cigarette.

"Look at how pretty your great-grandma was," she said, pointing at the center photograph with her forehead.

My great-grandmother was half of the middle couple and half the age of the grim man who gripped her shoulder. The man was balding. A razor-burned face folded into a grimace. His hands were large, and he was very tall and muscular. My great-grandmother, on the other hand, was small. Delicately boned. Her cheeks were flushed and her smile was shy. She had no idea what was coming next.

My mother couldn't look away. She stared at the photograph for a long time. Her eyes were dark and keen and shining. As though her pupils had nearly swallowed her irises. Had they always looked like that?

"She was very pretty," I said, rinsing out the pan.

My mother sighed. "She stayed long enough to have my father and my aunt. Raised them long enough to keep them out of danger. In those days on the farm, a mother could breathe easy once a child turned five. That's when they knew their baby would probably continue to live. A week after my aunt turned five, my grandmother stayed up all night baking enough bread and meat pies and stewing pots of beans to keep everyone fed for at least two weeks. She wrote out instructions on how to turn the cheeses and how to prepare the jars of salt pork and how to preserve the food in the garden. How to keep the mice out of the flour bin. How to keep the sourdough happy. How to keep everyone fed through the winter. Then she went outside. Paused one moment to wave goodbye. And then? She flew away. Just like that." My mother pressed one hand to her heart. The other she brought to her lips and blew the woman in the photograph a kiss.

I frowned.

"That's not what I heard, Mom," I said. "I heard that she hopped in a boxcar and didn't get out until she made it to San Francisco, where she lived a few years totally strung out, and died in a brothel or a drug house or on the street. Probably the street." People in town were always very quick to share with me what they thought they knew about my family's history.

My mother shook her head. "No. That's just a story," she said. "This town has always liked to invent wild tales. No one hopped boxcars in those days. And San Francisco was expensive then. Also, that story is irredeemably sexist, which makes it immediately suspect. Brothel, *my eye*." She rested her cheek on her hand. Kept her eyes fixed on the photograph. "I know what really happened. My father was there and he saw it, and he never forgot. She flew away. She was his mother and then . . . she wasn't. She was a flash of downy white, leaving the farm behind. Feathers and wings and all. And sky for days." She slid her gaze to the ground. "Lucky broad."

14.

Later that same night, after Michael was asleep, I walked out of the house, under the stars. There was a party that night, on the other side of town. I could have gone through the bother of sneaking out of my bedroom window, the way the other kids did when they surreptitiously made their way out, past curfew, heading toward a tangle of bad booze, bad music, and bad choices. Kids whose parents checked their homework and tucked them in and made sure there was something other than old condiments in the refrigerator. Kids who weren't me. For my part, I could have left the front door wide open, and my mom would not have noticed that I had gone. My mom and the crane sat at the kitchen table, saying nothing, looking at nothing. I walked right past them and out the door, under the roof of stars. They didn't notice me at all.

I wasn't much of a "go to parties" kind of kid, to be honest, and never really saw the point of getting particularly close to anyone at my high school. I can hardly remember their faces. But there was going to be a bonfire, which sounded okay, and I knew there would be food as well, along with the terrible liquor, and I was hungry. Plus, I figured I could stash something in my deep jacket pockets to bring home for Michael.

The stars were bright and the grass was wet and the sentinel drones hummed across the fields. The humid air from the day before had condensed into a deep night chill. I shivered under my father's old field jacket. I should have put on a sweater as well.

Kids massed in an abandoned lot on the other side of town, sandwiched between the old grain elevator and the remains of an ancient pork-processing plant—abandoned before my mother was even born. The lot had tall grasses, already tamped down by a crush of teenagers (and a few creepy adult hangers-on). A bonfire glowed in the center, surrounded by faces, mostly familiar and garishly lit. The remains of an abandoned hobo camp sat heaped in a corner. The farm conglomerate had pressured the town to empty those encampments a few weeks earlier—that happened a lot during the run-up to planting season. They claimed it was for safety reasons, but everyone knew it really was an attempt to avoid any potential bad publicity if their "smart" drone plowing system accidentally tore a person apart when that person didn't know to stay out of the field. Supposedly, those plows all have automatic stops if they detect something alive and moving in their path. But we had all seen the plowed-up remains of coyotes and foxes and birds littering the fields, and we all knew better.

The party was as boring as I assumed it would be. Dull music blared on raspy speakers while a bunch of boys from the baseball team set off fireworks (pointed toward the old grain elevator and not the fields—if they accidentally hit one of the conglomerate's drones, we'd all be in trouble). The bonfire was warm and bright, but the wood they burned had been treated with something that made the fire glow with strange colors and kicked out fumes that gave me a headache. I took my drink and headed over to the edge of the field, where I leaned back on an old tarp, pleasantly buzzed, and looked out at the glinting stars as a boy with a letterman's jacket sidled close and ran his hand along my thigh, back and forth. It was cold, and he was warm, and I figured why not. He was in my history class, and I couldn't for the life of me remember his name. I still can't. I was pretty sure it had only one syllable. Jack, maybe? Or Gus. He leaned his forehead just above my ear and told me about the drones that he and his teammates had commandeered and repurposed, mostly using them to spy on other teams and learn their secrets. Which seemed a lot of work for something that didn't matter much. He also told me about the plane he was going to build someday to fly around the world. He droned on and on. I didn't encourage him either way, but I'll admit that it was comforting, just the damp, warm, earnest presence of him, and I wasn't quite ready to go home yet. I kept my eyes out on the fields. There were more drones than usual—plowing day was coming soon. Their lights hovered in the dark, moving back and forth, back and forth, devouring the world with their eyes.

I found myself thinking about the man in the sheep pen in January. The man who had somehow gotten injured by one of those drones. The one who started my mother's mooning and sighing. If he had never shown up in the first place, would my mother have ever fallen for that stupid crane? I figured probably not. The drones hummed through the air. I tilted my head. They stayed higher than a man. And they weren't even that big. How on earth had he gotten so injured anyway? It still didn't make any sense.

I looked at the boy. He had been talking for a good twenty minutes at that point. I hadn't been paying attention for quite a lot of it.

"Hey," I said.

I think it was the first time I used my voice at all during that entire interaction. He was so startled, he removed his hand from my thigh. "Sorry," he said. "Oh my gosh. Super sorry. Is this not okay?"

I waved him off. "It's fine. I really don't care. You can do what you want. But I have a question for you."

He didn't take this as an invitation to replace his hand, and he seemed somewhat downtrodden by the fact of my question. I think he wanted to get back to his story. I continued anyway. "Do you still have those drones? The ones that you stole and repurposed."

The boy remained startled. "What?" He looked at me strangely, as though it hadn't occurred to him that I knew how to talk. Or that I had actually absorbed anything that he had said. Did he think that girls were empty vessels? Possibly. "The drones? Well, sure. We still have a couple. There's one in the truck."

"Is your truck here? Like, right now?"

"Sure," he said, utterly perplexed. "It's right over there." He pointed to the mess of cars on the other side of the abandoned lot.

I nodded. "Great." I pulled myself to my knees and took his hand. "Let's go over there and get it."

His eyebrows went up, and his cheeks began to flush. "You want to . . . *oh*." He pulled me closer. "Oh, I see now.

You want . . ." He leaned in close. He lowered his voice suggestively. "You want to see *inside of my truck*?" He burrowed his face into the curve of my neck.

"Nope," I said, pulling away. I stood and smiled at him, bright and hard and sharp. Like a star. "Not at all. I mean. You can stay in your truck if you want. Or you can stay here. Either way. I just need the drone. Where are your keys?"

Baffled, the boy led me to his truck, and even more baffled, he handed me the repurposed drone.

"Does it still work?" I asked.

"Yeah," he said. "They're stupid easy to hack. I think Horace is in charge of their security systems and he really sucks at it." He showed me the spot inside that needed a quick knock to scramble its connection to the central hub. The one port that needed to be cut. And then how to connect it to my own phone so I could navigate it with my maps. All told it took five minutes. He slid his arm around my waist as I examined the drone. A look of honey on his face. His fingers found their way under my shirt. "So," he said, moving closer. His breath in my hair. His hand awkwardly on my breast. "Don't you want to . . . I mean . . . you know . . . since we're here . . . and you're so pretty. I have a blanket in the back seat. We could, um, do something." He traced his hand toward the truck's interior like a waiter showing customers to their seats.

"Not at all," I said cheerfully. "But thanks for the drone . . . Mark?"

"That's not even my name," he said. "I've introduced myself to you like a hundred times. Do you really not remember?"

I hoisted the drone to my chest and wrapped my arms around it. "Well," I said, "nice meeting you again." And I walked home without looking back.

He wasn't kidding—not only were the drones stupid easy to connect, they were also a snap to use. Which made sense, since Horace was in charge of them. I sat out on the roof, sending it out on missions and watching what it watched through the viewer on my screen. I sent it into the sheep pen and along the border of the farm.

I sent it over to my mother's studio. The door was locked, but the window was open and the curtains were parted. It couldn't go all the way in, so I pointed the camera to look in through the metal screen. I couldn't see much. It was a mess in there. Heaps of clothing and debris. A broken chair. A desk covered with thick spilled paint, dotted with feathers. Piles of used tissues soaked with blood. The tapestry hung on the far wall. I couldn't get a clear view. But something about it made my skin crawl. I didn't know why.

I redirected the drone back toward the house, checking on the sheep again (they were fine), and then let it hover just outside of my mother's room. I repositioned the view.

"Oh," I whispered.

Her curtains were open, and the room was a riot of feathers. They heaped on the floor and crowded the closet. Her antique vanity table (originally a wedding gift to some great-grandmother or other) was completely buried. Her drawers exploded with feathers. My mother lay in bed, a sheet wrapped around her body like a shroud. She was fast asleep. A man lay next to her. Fully nude. His arms and legs spread out. Like he owned the place. I zoomed in on his face. It was the man from the sheep pen.

But of course it was.

I checked the time. It was 2:54. I looked closer at my mother. There were bruises on her shoulders. Across her back. A sizable cut behind her ear. Deep gouges on her legs. All easy to cover up. Hide the wounds. He avoided her face. I didn't know then that such strategies are unsurprising. I only know that now.

I readjusted the drone's position and view and looked more closely at her face. Her cheeks continued to thin. So did her hair, which looked as though it were coming out in clumps. She wasn't okay, I realized with a sharp constriction in my throat. And it was while I was staring at my mom that the clock slid from 2:59 to 3:00. The bed shuddered. The man gasped. And

Oh! The elongated neck. And

Oh! The protrusion of his lips—from pillows, to pincers, to blades. And

Oh! The explosion of feather and claw. And

Oh! How his eyes became wide, then astonished, then livid. How his eyes, green as cornstalks, became red, then black, then *keen, keen, keen.* He opened his beak. He opened his wings. His voice transformed from a man's mournful cry to a bird's panicked screech with no moment in between. One becomes the other becomes one. Perhaps it was all the same from the beginning. The man is the crane is the man.

My mom woke up. She curled toward the bird, her hands on his face. I could see her speaking quickly, her fingers caressing his feathers. Soothing. As though he were a child. The crane reared back, the tip of his beak arcing toward the ceiling. It swiveled forward, all speed and ferocity, like an overcranked spring, smacking her hard on the side of her head, cutting her scalp. I saw my mother press her hands into her hair. I saw her cower protectively, in the fetal position, as the crane unfolded himself from the bed and headed to the door. I saw him leave without looking back.

Oh, I said to myself, once my mind became quiet. *I understand.*

15.

What did I do with that information? What could I do?

If I'm being honest? Nothing.

I didn't tell my teachers.

I didn't tell the social worker.

I didn't tell anyone.

What could I even say, anyway? My family had told stories of women becoming birds since before my mother was born. They filled my mother's head with them. No one was supposed to believe them. I certainly didn't. They were just stories. There were other possibilities for what might have happened to those women that were far more logical. The persistent rumors, for example, cataloged in town about the indiscreet choices made by the women in my family—mothers losing their grip on morals and sanity and respectability, running away to dens of sex or drugs and dying of things too terrible to name—seemed far more plausible.

And yet.

I never told anyone about what my mother did with her time and attention. Why would I? It was no one's business but ours. I also never told anyone that I was the one who took care of my baby brother—that I was the one who fed him, bathed him, dressed him, and measured the medicine when he was sick. It was a family matter, after all. I never told anyone that I was the one who cooked the dinner and balanced the checkbook and made sure buyers paid what they owed. I was the one who called the light company, begging for an extension. I never told anyone about the strangers who came in and out of our house. The things they did. The crane wasn't the first to give her cuts and bruises. He was just the first to stick around long enough to give her this many.

My mom was sleeping with a crane who was sometimes a man. Or a man who was sometimes a crane. My mom was sleeping with a person who hit her. Both of these things felt too awful—too *wrong*—to talk about. So who would I tell? There was no one to tell. So I told no one.

Instead, I did what I always did. I took care of Michael. I praised him for his schoolwork and I took him on walks along the road and sometimes we went looking for frogs (not to bring home, obviously; too dangerous, poor little things). I drew with him and sang to him and sometimes he helped me with our sheep. He was too thin. Too light. Mom needed to make money. We needed more groceries. But I didn't know how to ask for that either. What if the social worker came back? What if she didn't like what she saw? What if someone took Michael away? What then?

I continued flying the drone at night. Watching. I tried using it to see into my mother's studio while she and the crane worked for hours and hours. But she kept the curtains drawn and the door locked. I could see only their shadows in the evenings when the lamps were lit and the sky grew dark. I could see only my mother's silhouette at the loom or the two of them dancing around and around and around. I couldn't make sense of it. I didn't understand until it was too late.

I landed the drone on the roof of the barn, its nose and main camera focused on the yard. I had footage of the crane-as-man wandering out at night. Always without clothes. He menaced the sheep. He pulled frogs out of the pond and ate them whole. He lay on the grass and stared up at the sky. I didn't know what he wanted. I didn't care. I just wanted him gone.

A week went by. I took notes. I made diagrams. I even made a chart. I tried to hide all of this from Michael, who followed me from room to room with his wide, sober eyes. I did what I could to keep him fed. I did what I could to keep the house clean and orderly in case the social worker came back. I couldn't protect my mother from the crane, and I wasn't sure if I would even be able to protect myself, but I sure as hell would protect Michael. The crane would not touch him. I used my body as a shield, moving Michael out of the room whenever the crane sauntered in, always putting myself in between, like a wall.

One evening, my mother took Michael by the hand, and they both went upstairs to read stories. I stayed in the kitchen to wash the dishes.

After a while, the crane walked in. He finally got rid of the shoes, but he still wore the spectacles and the hat. He sauntered across the living room and paused at the kitchen. He adjusted his feathers as he looked me up and down. I purposefully ignored him and returned to the soapy water, enjoying for a moment the heat and bubbles. I could feel the crane staring at the back of my body, his gaze like needles in my skin. I turned my face slightly so he could see my scowl, and in the corner of my eye I saw a man.

That man.

I jumped.

Screamed.

Grabbed the nearest cooking pot and whirled around, brandishing it over my head like a machete.

Except it wasn't a man at all. It was the crane. I shook my head and blinked hard. It was the man again. No. It was definitely the crane. He flickered back and forth—man, not-man; crane, not-crane. He didn't move except to move from one state to the other. Was he enjoying this? He seemed to be enjoying this. He smiled, showing his missing teeth. Panic still thumping in my chest, I expelled my breath in a quiet, *Oh.* I closed my eyes tight for a moment or two. When I opened them, the crane stood in the exact same spot, fully a crane. Like he was daring me to comment. Cranes have beaks and cannot grin, and yet he seemed to anyway. The crane leered at me. His eyes were everywhere.

"*Go away,*" I hissed at him.

He squawked suggestively.

"I don't want you to be here anymore," I said with more force. I grabbed a wet dish towel and threw it right at his face. It hung there, wet and dripping, from the length of his cruel beak. He didn't even flinch. He said nothing, not even a squawk, but I still heard his silent *Baby, I ain't going nowhere* as though he had shouted it.

I turned on my heel and left the dishes in the sink and marched to my room. I threw the window open and crawled out onto the roof, lying out on the pitch, watching the sun set over the fields. The drones buzzed and the plows rumbled and the sheep complained and birds skirted the edges of the crops, launching high overhead to avoid the mechanical sentinels moving back and forth, back and forth.

And that's when I realized that I could no longer wait for the crane to leave on his own accord. If I wanted to get rid of him, I would have to do it myself.

16.

My high school, overnight, became a cacophony of prom paraphernalia. Signs and posters and streamers and insufferably annoying public declarations of intent. Kids arranged dance routines and a cappella arrangements and once a parade of tiny flying drones, each carrying a rose (that kid got suspended: drones were appropriate on farmland, but *not* on school property).

The boy from the party (Mark? Alex? Randy? Gus? I couldn't remember—even an hour after the party I couldn't remember) asked me to be his prom date in the middle of the lunchroom, as his friends from track knelt while snapping and humming a song from *West Side Story,* which just felt inappropriate.

"Does this have to be in public?" I asked, my eyes darting at the faces staring at me. Because they knew who I was. And they knew who my mother was. I wasn't the sort of girl that nice boys ask to the prom. No one in my family ever was. The spectators at the lunch tables looked on with a narrowed gaze. Arms crossed. Lips pressed. *Who does she think she is?* No one said this. But their faces shouted it all the same. One girl rolled her eyes. I regarded the boy. It wasn't kind, what I had to do, and I felt bad about it. He was a nice enough boy, looking at me with this dopey sweetness. I sighed and shook my head.

"Okay," I said. "Fine. Then publicly, no. I won't go to prom with you. I'm frankly astonished that you thought I'd say yes. Now don't you wish you could have done this quietly?"

He stood, brushed the floor dust off of his knees, called me a bitch and so did two of his friends, but that was okay with me. I'm sure other people called me worse things, under their breath. I had already been asked, less publicly, three other times earlier, but my answer was the same. I don't know what they were expecting. I wasn't a prom sort of kid.

Later that day, my math teacher told me that I was supposed to report to the office.

"What for?" I asked. I didn't actually care, since it meant I got to leave class. I had already slung my bag over my shoulder and I was in the process of heading toward the door. My curiosity was more reflexive than anything else.

The teacher shrugged and started handing back the quiz from the day before. I took that as my cue to make myself scarce so I didn't have to see what I had gotten. I didn't have high hopes.

When I arrived at the office, the secretary sent me to the back room, where the principal sat with the social worker lady who had come to my house earlier. Her hair was still piled and secured on top of her head in a pleasant mound. She still wore the glasses with the green lights flashing at the tips. She smiled.

"I'm legally required to tell you that I'm recording this interaction," she said with cheerful precision.

"Yeah," I said, looking from one to the other. "You don't have to tell me that every time. I already know what your glasses are for."

The principal was a dour man who wore heavy sweaters even when it was warm out. He didn't look at me but rather turned his attention to picking at his cuticles. He often told the class that the purpose of the school was to help those who chose to help themselves. I was obviously one that he didn't much care to bother with since I clearly wasn't doing much to help myself. He moved on to his next finger. He didn't have anything to say.

The social worker opened up her folder. "Your mother was supposed to be here. She was called. She was emailed. We sent her letters in the mail. And yet she saw fit not to attend."

I shrugged. "Well, she's busy."

The social worker looked me in the eye, a sharp, insistent gaze. "Is she now? With what?"

I dropped my eyes to the table. "You know how it goes," I mumbled. "Artists. . . ." My voice trailed off.

"Yes," she said slowly. "Artists."

I kept my gaze on my folded hands.

We sat silently for a moment. The clock on the wall ticked loudly. From somewhere in a nearby hallway, two boys shouted and grunted. There was the distinctive sound of a fist hitting a face, always louder than you'd expect. I flinched.

The social worker cleared her throat. "And it looks like Bruce has been by since I saw you last."

This startled me. My head flicked up. "What?" I said.

The social worker innocently busied herself with her

paperwork. "Oh, you know," she said. "I like to keep up on the local arts. I subscribed to his newsletter."

I wrote the newsletter, obviously. Usually I sent one out to the subscribers only once or twice a year. When Mom was getting ready to sell a piece. But I had been panicking about Mom's income, so I sent two out in succession to get potential buyers keyed up to hopefully start a bidding war. I hadn't seen the piece, obviously—only glimpses. So I used the most hyperbolic and outlandish language I could think of. The tapestry was a complex wonder, I wrote, a baffling reassessment of both time and space, an enigmatic refutation of the mundane. I described how it made nuns throw their rosaries in the trash and made hardened criminals see God. It was the intersection of Being and Unbeing, Knowing and Unknowing, an infinite journey into the mouth of the Universe. And other garbage. I can't even remember all of it. I just hit send. The subscribers *ate it up.* People responded with heartfelt praise and ridiculous emojis and congratulatory animations. I had twelve offers to buy it sight unseen. At prices that made my jaw drop. I showed these to my mother, but she wouldn't hear of it.

"Oh," I said, still not looking up, trying to force away the creeping blush in my neck and cheeks. "That's, um, pretty cool. I . . . don't think I knew he made a newsletter." I swallowed. "Good old Bruce," I added weakly.

The social worker's face didn't alter at all. "One could say that," she demurred. "Look, I have it right here." She pulled up the newsletter on her tablet but didn't show it to me. Instead she scrolled through it like it was the most compelling literature to ever cross her desk.

"Anything interesting?" I managed.

The social worker cocked her head. She gave me a *look*. But she let it slide. "Bruce posted pictures of the sheep. One of them looks sick, poor thing. Your mother should call the vet. And look over here. It's an older photo of your mom at her loom—I recognized it from an earlier year. Nothing recent of her, I notice. Or of you. But there are several of your brother. Here he is painting the barn. Here he is climbing a tree—an obvious danger. Here he is wading in the pond with no visible adult supervising him, which was frankly alarming. And there over by the barn is a disconcertingly large bird. Personally, I blame the weird chemicals that they spray on those fields. Are you sure it's safe having a bird that large near a child that small?" She darkened the screen of her tablet and set it on the table. "Bruce certainly does like taking pictures of your little brother, doesn't he? Honey, I think we need to talk about that. Who is this man again? If he's an employee, I'm certain that your mother did a background check, right? Since he comes in contact with her children. *Her children.* Does he come by often?"

"Not really. He just came to bring . . . some supplies. You know. For the art. And to pick up his payment. Because he is definitely an employee."

"Is he? Are you sure? He's not listed. We have your mother's financials—"

"Sorry. Volunteer." I smiled. "And. You know. A what's-it-called. A gig worker. My mom pays him in cash because he hates banks." This was true of my mom as well.

The social worker sighed deeply. She rested her forehead briefly on her fingertips and then pressed her hands together.

"Listen," she said. "The county is cracking down on

truant youth. If you were a senior, then everyone would assume you're a lost cause and wouldn't care. The system wouldn't get involved. But you aren't a senior. You are *fifteen*. Which means that we do care." She closed the folder. "*I* care."

The principal still hadn't said a damn thing. He scrolled through his phone. He quietly guffawed every once in a while.

The social worker cleared her throat. She took off her glasses and looked at me full in the face. "When a parent doesn't answer a single phone call, and doesn't respond to repeated attempts to reach her—including home visits! In the middle of the day! And I absolutely know she saw me standing there, and I *do not know what* was going on in that barn, but I am *not* happy about it—then we get worried. Since you and I last spoke you've missed six more classes."

"Not six," I said. "My teachers aren't being truthful." It was definitely six. Actually it likely was at least ten, but my art teacher wasn't great at taking attendance.

"I take offense at that," the principal said. He still didn't look up. He kept his eyes on his phone, scrolling, scrolling. He looked at the clock. Then: "Sorry, ladies, I have to take this." He stood and left the room. He brought his phone, which had not rung, to his ear. "Hello?" he said to no one. He closed the door behind him.

"I think your teachers are being truthful," the social worker said briskly. She put her folder into her bag. "And I think they are furthermore being truthful when they tell me that you're smart, and capable, and that you've been dealt a bad hand. That you could have a bright future ahead of you if you only seize it."

"My hand is fine." I crossed my arms across my chest. I didn't want to look at her anymore. I didn't want her to look at *me*. "And my future will be what it will be. It's not like anyone can predict any of that stuff anyway." I know I was being a sullen teenager. I knew it then. But I didn't care.

She sighed. "Well, Mr. Patterson has seen fit not to return, which means this meeting has to end. Rules are rules." She stood and opened the door, keeping her body visible to anyone who might walk by. She paused a moment, as though working out what it was that she wanted to say. "I'm going to tell you something, and I want you to listen, because it's important: If something feels wrong at home, if you think people aren't safe, if you think that someone is making others unsafe, you have a responsibility to say something." She paused. Her eyes were grave. "Do you understand what I'm saying? A *responsibility*. You don't have a responsibility to solve it—you can't. You're only a kid. You can't solve anything on your own. But there are systems in place that are designed to solve these problems. You can be the catalyst that sets those systems in motion—the spark that starts the engine. Or you can sit by and allow yourself to be a victim. You have a choice here. Do you understand?"

I looked at her. I knew what happened to kids when they got pulled into those systems. And I knew that if that happened, there was no way Michael and I would be allowed to stay together. How could we? A cute, big-eyed six-year-old would have a hell of a lot easier time being placed in a family if he wasn't saddled with his truant, fifteen-year-old sister. I wasn't an idiot. I knew how these things went.

And I needed to take care of Michael. It was my job.

I needed to take care of my mom. I had promised Dad.

Who was I if I didn't have them?

"I understand perfectly," I said. I tried to be kind. I think I was. "I appreciate your help. I really do."

I smiled for the camera.

The social worker nodded, turned on her heel, and walked out of the office.

17.

It was a delicate business, obviously. With moving parts. Every action necessarily causes a reaction, and if you're not prepared for it, the blowback can knock you flat, undo everything you attempted to set in motion. Or worse, leave you in a worse place than you started.

Or a different place.

Sometimes it's tough to tell the difference.

I had known enough kids who had gotten swooped up in the caring, well-meaning, but often overcompensating talons of the social services agencies that served our town. Siblings split apart. Parents unmoored without their children, making worse choices than the ones that got them into that mess in the first place.

What I knew was this: my mother needed me; my brother needed me; and I needed them both. These were truths that were both self-evident and irrefutable. I knew that farmhouse was ours and had always been ours. And it *needed* to be ours. Each photograph with each long-gone generation attested to it, grim-faced men, all. I knew that my mom needed to do her art and that Michael needed my mom. These were the threads that tethered us all to the ground. Break just one, and we would go hurling into the vacuum of space. I don't know how I knew this. But I did.

I thought about my mom's fervent belief that women on the farm sprouted wings and flew away. If it was true (and I wasn't entirely convinced), then what had caused it? She said that they waited until their children were five and out of danger, and then they flew away from the farm. *From the farm.* But then, when I was five my dad got sick. And he stayed sick. And when Michael was five my dad was already gone, and there was no one to take care of us. Is that why she stayed? Or was it the farm itself that made the mothers change? Which was an interesting theory, since the farm wasn't ours. Not anymore. No one person owned the farm. No one walked the farm. The farm belonged to machines and shareholders. No one loved it anymore. No one was tied to it anymore. The only things that flew across it were drones with their cold, electric eyes. There was nothing to fly away from. No feathers. No wings. Only a memory of the farm as it used to be—a place we could see but couldn't touch. Perhaps that was why she couldn't fly away.

I shook my head. It was a moot point. No one was flying anywhere, except maybe that crane.

But there were details to attend to first.

I sat in my room, listening to my mother sing to Michael. Her voice was thin and fragile as winter grass. Michael asked for song after song. When the singing stopped, I knew he had fallen asleep. I listened for her footsteps down the hall, but those were harder to pick up. She had lost so much weight. She was a shadow of herself. She barely made a sound on the floorboards. I heard the sound of a body being slammed to the wall. My mom gasped. A nervous giggle.

She said, "I'm working on it. I swear I'm working on it."

A scratching sound. A thud.

She said, "Baby, I want this as much as you do. Surely you know that now."

A sharp slap. A muffled cry.

"Tomorrow, I think." Her words were muted, as though she were speaking into her hand. "We'll know if I'm on the right track with this approach tomorrow. Then I'll follow the stitches, follow the thread. Just like always. I have a good feeling. It *wants to be,* you know?"

Another voice grunted. A low *hmmm.* I looked at my watch. It was midnight. He was a man again. In my mind's eye, I could see him lifting her into his arms. I could see her wrapping her arms around his neck. Nuzzling his cheek. Blood on his stubble. Blood in his hair. He carries her to the bedroom and shuts the door with the smile of his heel. He throws her onto the bed with a quiet heave.

For a while, at least, they wouldn't be thinking about the art in my mother's studio.

But I was.

I stood. Crept out of my room. Tiptoed down the hall and out into the yard. My mother moaned. The crane grunted. Or a man, I suppose. When he was a man, was he not also the crane? When he was the crane, was he not also the man? It didn't matter. He'd be gone soon enough.

I couldn't use the drone. The windows were closed, the shades down. But I could use my camera. And I had some tools in a box that I hadn't used in a long time.

I made my way toward the barn. The sheep saw me

but fortunately kept their mouths shut. They had been so muted lately—sullen and lethargic and depressed. Off their food. I didn't know how much longer they could carry on this way. Especially Nix. She was too old for this kind of stress.

At the studio door, I set my toolbox on the ground and knelt beside it.

And then I started picking the lock.

It took longer than I remembered, but I finally coaxed the pins into place and disengaged the spring. It gave way with a satisfying click, making my head rush. I pushed open the door.

"*Oh,*" I whispered, pressing my hands to my heart. My breath caught, and stuttered, and my voice tangled in my throat, as though my soul were escaping in sighs. I stepped into the studio, not knowing where to look first. I fell to my knees, overwhelmed, crowded by my mother's brutal, unmerciful beauty. "*Oh, my.*"

I took out my phone. And I started taking pictures.

18.

The day my dad died, I sat in my mother's studio, refusing to come out. My mother banged on the door for what felt like a long time but probably was only a minute or two. She stopped after a while, complaining that it hurt her hand.

"I'm going to go and sit with Daddy," she said through the door. "With his body. Me and Michael and Daddy. Us together. You should hurry. There's other people coming, too, probably. And soon. This town, honey, it's filled with vultures. But I won't let them in until you come. You need to come and sit, my darling. You need to be present with Daddy this one last time. It matters. You'll be too sad later if you miss your chance."

I sat in the center of the room. Her desk was to my left. Her loom to my right. A complicated spinning wheel in the corner. I sat cross-legged on the floor. A basket filled with skeins of thread and yarn had tipped over, spilling its contents over my feet. I didn't really understand what my mother did. I knew that she drew. I knew that she turned the sheep's wool into string. And I knew that she took the ideas from her head and the feelings in her heart and the thread on the skeins and somehow turned them into a giant story that hung from the ceiling and spilled all the way down the wide wall onto the floor.

My father told me that weavers were magic.

My mother wasn't magic.

And yet. The idea did seem a little bit magic.

I looked at my mother's drawings. There were so many on the desk that they gathered and massed into piles and drifted onto the ground like leaves. There were figures in her drawings that looked like Michael and me—riding on boats made of flowers or climbing up the necks of giant cornstalks or chasing after flying sheep. There was a drawing of my dad. He was halfway buried in the ground, his arms stretched up and holding on to a bird as it desperately tried to fly away. The expression on my father's face—panicked, pleading, an expression of sorrow and longing. I looked at the bird, its beak wide open, its one anguished, livid eye.

I went to the fabric hanging from the ceiling. It was huge and garbled and unfinished. I could see the children in flower boats floating across a river filled with trash (there was actual trash, stitched into the story). I could see the beginnings of the bird, constructed with actual feathers stitched onto the fabric. The figure of the man was merely outlined at that point with a white chalk pencil. Off to the side, draped on another worktable was a figure of a man made of patchwork and covered with buttons. Clearly, my mother wasn't done.

My dad told me stories of weavers who stitched the world and spun fortunes and pulled on strings to change someone's fate. Was there a string I could pull to stop my father from dying? Was there a patch I could secure to block my mother from going away? I stared at the tapestry for a long time until finally I gave up.

There were no answers to be found.

I opened the door and went to sit with my mother and my brother. I held my father's hand as it slowly turned cold.

19.

My father had given me his tools before he died. Tools for carpentry or machines or general fixing. Specialized tools for the computer. Lockpicking tools. Curved needles to fix upholstery. An excellent knife for carving. A shotgun with an unknown purpose.

"What's that for?" I asked.

"Just in case," my father explained as he gravely placed it in my hands, though I didn't understand what that case might be.

He showed me the way an adult writes a letter and he showed me how to build a simple website. He showed me how a checkbook worked. And how to fix a vacuum cleaner. And how to swap the storm windows with the window screens. He gave me the tool of mathematics and the tool of understanding how a ledger worked and the tool of simply knowing how money worked. I tucked my box of tools under my arm. My father had told me, "One day you'll see that every vexing problem has a tool to set it right. Your mother doesn't understand this, which is why you will sometimes need to step in and take care of things for her. Make sure you know where your tools are."

"Yes, Daddy," I said.

"Your mother doesn't know these things," he said, a note of pleading in his voice. "She has always been that way. She is an artist. Her feet barely touch the ground. I've been the one to keep her tethered to the earth. And now it's your job. And you're too young, and it's not fair, but there it is."

He was right. It wasn't fair. But I didn't know it then, and I didn't even entirely know it as I carried the shotgun up from the basement, and opened the case on my bed. I know it now, though. But it's too late now to fix anything.

In my room, I carefully loaded the gun and hid it in my closet. Then I sat at my desk and uploaded the pictures I had taken of the tapestry onto my school-issued laptop, where I created a new page on my mother's website. The tapestry was too massive to capture in one image, and there was no way to communicate the scale. Instead I used words like "a 360° immersive experience" and "multidimensional storytelling" and "a heartbreaking exploration of broken women, broken communities, a broken world." I used words like "illuminating" and "transfixing" and "transcendent." None of these did the piece justice. I uploaded pictures of small details.

Mechanical men marching across a green field, leaving ruin in their wake.

A man with a woman's neck in his fist.

A house made of flower petals.

Another made of wheat.

And still another made from the yarn unwound from a baby's blanket.

Another man who seemed to be stitched almost entirely out of light.

A rabbit, made from strips of actual fur (I thought immediately of Goldilocks and Kublai Khan, poor things)—muscular legs, long, delicate ears, a fragile, searching nose—that went leaping into a fire that looked as though it were actually burning.

I didn't show them the central image. I couldn't even bring myself to take the picture. Even thinking about it spooked me. A woman who was a bird who was a woman. A man who was a crane who was a man. They flickered and changed. They became as large as the room. They were so small they could fit on a hand. They stood in a garden, under a tree. And watching them, I felt myself covered in feathers. And watching them, I felt myself grow wings. It was impossible, of course. They were just stitches on fabric. They couldn't *change*.

And yet.

Art, true art, exists only to transform, my mother had said. *And it is only truly art when it* does *transform. The maker. The viewer. Everyone.*

Did it transform her? Did it transform *me*? And if it did, could I stop it?

It took me nearly two hours, but I finished the auction page. I sent the link to the subscriber list. I set the time. My mother would balk at this, but we needed the money. This was her best work. And it was killing her. Best to send it to some dealer and have them suffer with it.

I hit the upload button and turned around and nearly screamed, because Michael stood by the door of my room. His eyes were large and frightened.

"Buddy," I said, nearly collapsing. "What on earth are you doing up?"

"There's a man in the house," he whispered.

I patted my legs and held out my arms. He climbed into the well of my lap and let me wrap my arms around him. I tried to rock him back and forth, but it was difficult. Michael was tense and panicked. He hiccuped and swallowed.

"What are you talking about?" I asked, trying to sound soothing.

"There's a man in the house," he said again. His voice was light and staccato as the sound moths make when they hit the hot glass of the floodlight out back. I tilted my head. I heard footsteps. I kept my face neutral, hoping that Michael wouldn't notice the increase in my heart rate. I looked at the clock. It was nearly three in the morning. If he was a man, he'd be a crane soon.

I couldn't shoot a man. But I sure as hell could shoot a damn bird.

"I don't think there's anything for you to worry about," I said. I stood. Pulled a sweatshirt over my tank top. Slid my feet into shoes. I smoothed his hair back and kissed his forehead. "You know that you'll always be able to count on me. No matter what. Right?"

He nodded. Wiped his running nose with the back of his hand.

I tucked him into my bed and told him to go to sleep. I told him not to move until I returned. I told him that I had the tools to fix this problem and he just needed to close his eyes and wait for everything to be fine. I told him I'd check every single room and that I'd make sure the doors were bolted. I told him I'd call the police if I saw anything. He smiled at me and curled into the covers, closing his eyes. I grabbed the shotgun from the back of my closet and carried it gingerly out of the room, pressing the button lock on my doorknob before closing the door behind me. It wouldn't really stop anyone who wanted to kick it down, but it certainly would slow them down.

I rested the barrel of the gun on my shoulder and listened.

My mother's voice in the yard. "I think this time. I think I have it all set."

A man's voice: "You thought that before."

My mother's voice: "But this time I'm right."

The barn door swung hard, slamming closed. I tore through the house at a run.

20.

There were feathers on the stairway. And feathers in the kitchen. And feathers in the hall. The back door was open. There were feathers on the porch. Feathers littering the backyard. They got in my mouth. They obscured my vision. They swirled and swarmed, catching the breeze. The drones hummed over the fields. From far away, I could hear the plows starting up. There had been signs up all week that they'd be planting our section soon. In theory, the machinery wasn't allowed to start before the sun came up because of the noise, but Horace always fired them up early to let them warm up for an hour or two. He said that's what his father used to do, back when his father used to farm. Anyone who wanted to complain could take it up with the conglomerate. Or they could complain to the corn—the response would be about the same either way.

The sheep bellowed from their pen, their eyes wild. Beverly reared up on her back legs. Nix turned in circles.

"Mom," I called out. *"Mom."*

I ran up the stairs and banged on the door to the studio.

"Nothing to worry about, my darling." My mother's voice seeped from under the door. It dripped down the walls. It flowed down the stairs, making me slip. "Go back to bed." Her voice was sticky on my skin. In my hair. It congealed on my fingertips.

"What's going on?" I yelled. I stood at the top of the stairs, my fists pounding the studio door.

Why must she be here? a man's voice whispered. In the air. At the window. It buzzed like a runaway drone over an endless field. *Nobody wants her here.*

Wings rustled. Fabric ripped. The sheep bellowed outside. I pounded on the door.

"Mom, let me in, *please*!" I shouted. "Mom, please open the door!"

You know about my mother, of course, my mom said. I didn't hear this with my ears. This wasn't her speaking voice. It was her voice in my head. *You know about my mother. She used to water down my father's whiskey just to make him inch into withdrawal—not enough to kill him, mind you, but just to make him sick enough to want to go to the hospital. She used to hide the horse tranquilizer and the diazepam for the sheep because he'd pop them like candy. She had a deep scar in her temple from when he put his boot in her face. And she was missing three teeth, thanks to his fist. He was never violent with us, even when she flew away—broken wings and all. She didn't make it far. Plow got her. I suppose her body is nothing but a row of cloned corn now. Is that what you want for me?*

"You're not your mother, Mom," I said. Who was I even talking to? No one was there. And yet. I felt my mom in my bones. I felt her in the air. I didn't have my tools with me. I threw my body against the door. I kicked and I kicked until the wood began to crack. "You're you. You belong to yourself. You belong to your art. You belong to me and Michael. We don't want you to fly away." I choked on my own sobs.

But that's what mothers do. On the farm. We sprout wings and fly away.

"Literally no one else's family is like that, Mom," I said. I kicked the door. Again and again.

Your father wasn't supposed to go first.

I kicked the door. The cracks deepened.

He got sick and slipped away from us and it was all wrong. It's mothers who leave the farm. Everyone knows that.

I kicked the door. The wood splintered.

Once upon a time, a girl fell in love with a swan. Or an eagle. Or a crane. It's all the same story, you know.

"It's not a story, Mom." My voice was ragged and raw. "This is real life."

The wood shattered and gave way. I forced my way in.

The light inside flickered. It was my mother and the crane. The light flickered. It was my mother and a man. The light flickered. It was a man and a crane. The light flickered. It was two cranes, one holding the other's neck in its beak.

"GIVE HER BACK," I roared. Was I talking to one crane or two? Was I talking to the man? Or was I talking to my mom? *"GIVE HER BACK THIS MINUTE."*

The smaller crane pulled away. She was so much smaller—a delicate beak, creamy feathers. She perched on the window. She was my mom, naked in the moonlight. She was the bird, a mournful cry in her throat. And then she was my mother again. "This is all wrong," she said, sobbing.

I braced the shotgun in the crook of my arm. My mother

was a bird and a woman and a bird. The crane was a man and the crane and a man. I couldn't shoot a man. But I could shoot that goddamned bird. I held him in my eye, breathed slow, and waited for my moment.

The bulb popped and we were in darkness. A man laughed. A crane screeched. Something sharp sliced my cheek and stabbed at my side. I stumbled forward and felt a hand, felt feathers, felt the impact of something large and heavy against my skull. A laugh. A squawk. I aimed through the darkness. I heard a crane's keen and I pulled the trigger. And then I felt nothing at all.

21.

Baked crane, even if you roast low and slow—and also stuff it with the onions and carrots from the root cellar that you once grew in the garden out back—just isn't very good. It's stringy and tough and—well, *rude* isn't a flavor, per se, but if it was, this meat would taste *rude*.

Still.

Food was food. And we were hungry.

My mother taught me well. I know how to pluck and gut a bird. I know how to use a resource when a resource presents itself. I know how to alter and augment, how to make scraps into a meal. I know how to hoard the things that will protect my family. These are skills you don't un-learn.

Michael and I ate through the leftover crane meat for the next three weeks. Drumsticks first, then wings, then shredded over rice, then in sandwiches, then dressed up with mayonnaise and spread on crackers. We boiled the bones for stock and had soup for days.

"You're sure it's not Mom?" Michael asked me a thousand times after I explained what had happened that night. And then another thousand after that.

"I'm *positive*. It's definitely, you know." I swallowed. Already it was getting hard to talk about. The day was coming soon when we would never speak of it again. Both Michael and I knew this in our bones. "It's, well. The crane. The one that Mom wanted us to call 'Father' but was *not* our father. That crane. Who, by the way, was *mean*."

I added that to justify it to myself, more than anything else. I had told myself that I would never shoot a man. I wasn't sure if he was a man when I shot him. When I got the lights back on, he was very much a crane and very much dead. And I am my mother's child. And my mother was a farmer's daughter. We both know how to be ruthlessly practical. I didn't even question what would happen next. I just did it. So it goes.

"Besides," I added, "he was wearing that stupid hat." This wasn't exactly true. The hat was *near* the bird. Near enough. And anyway, the dead crane on the studio floor was big. Taller than Mom. And his feathers were gray, not startlingly white, the way Mom's . . . I mean. I definitely shot *that* crane. The correct crane.

"As long as you're sure," Michael said as he ate another sandwich.

For days, Michael and I said nothing to anyone about what had happened. We went to school—or he went to school after I dropped him off and then I went home. I cleaned the house. Scrubbed the studio. Removed every single indication that a crane had lived here—the shoes with talon holes, the hat, the feathers that permeated every room in the house. I spent time with the sheep.

The auction for my mother's tapestry still had several days left, but the bidding was more anemic than I would have liked. Perhaps my descriptions were too outlandish. Perhaps because I couldn't get the whole scope of my mother's endeavor into my camera's lens. So I called off the sale, apologizing to those who had bid. Said my mother realized that she had more details that she needed to add and wasn't ready to let go quite yet.

"Artists," I said in my email. "What can you do?" I signed it "Bruce."

Two days later, I started planting rumors and suggestions on various chat rooms and message boards—using several aliases, of course—that my mother had been murdered.

Or she had gone into hiding.

Or that someone was after her.

Or she had simply disappeared.

A scorned lover, I wrote on one forum.

The farming conglomerate, I wrote on another.

She saw something that she shouldn't have, and They can't stand it, I wrote on a conspiracy theorist site.

This town never did like her kind, I intimated to a sympathetic reading public.

I put nothing on my mother's website. "Bruce" stopped responding to questions.

But the rumors spread. Crowdsourced donation sites appeared. Memorial compilation videos proliferated online, thousands opening all at once, like dandelions. The more people thought there was a chance that she might be dead, the more interest in her work increased. Sometimes, people are depressingly predictable.

In the meantime, I started photographing and sorting and boxing up everything I could find and announced a new sale. I built a beautiful auction site, with a picture of my mother at the center. She was in her wedding dress (already bulging with the beginnings of me), flowers in her hair and her face uptilted toward the sky. Thumbnails of her work crowded the next page. I made labels. I created a master list of asking prices for starting bids. I put everything I could find up for sale. The paintings she had made on old barnwood and discarded in the basement. Needlepoint pillows and yards of handwoven fabrics. The dress she intricately embroidered and wore when she won some award. A box of sketchbooks. The throw blankets with shadow cities hiding in the stitches and wall hangings crammed with forests and futuristic neighborhoods and subterranean worlds—all experiments that she abandoned and repurposed—that filled our house. I made a separate page for the final tapestry and set a starting bid so high the number made me gasp—and was astonished when the numbers came in and increased almost immediately. I even, with a great sadness in my heart, took out an ad to sell our three sheep. I couldn't look them in the eye after I had done it.

It's for Michael, I told myself as the sheep plaintively baaed in my direction. *This is all for Michael.*

The rumors about my mother's health, safety, and whereabouts continued to swirl, even as the auction proceeded. Was she alive? Was she dead? People emailed Bruce and asked.

"The family appreciates privacy during this time," I

wrote back, adding, "Please restrict your questions and comments to the auction only. Thanks. Bruce."

Outside auction houses tried to get involved, of course, but I wasn't going to hand over a single cent of my mother's earnings to anyone. I handled the sale. Sent confidentiality agreements to all potential buyers. Took credit card numbers and notarized statements of intent and removal. I could have asked them for the moon if I wanted to. I put the proceeds into a trust account that I had set up for Michael, so that no one—not a foster parent or a court-appointed guardian or even an adopted family—would be able to touch it until he turned eighteen. We had no family outside of one another, and there was no chance we would be kept together in the foster system. Not with my truancy and social services file. Not with Michael's youth and sweetness. They would want to give him the best start possible, unweighted by his unfortunate big sister.

After the tapestry sold and the movers the buyer hired carted it away (two of them broke down weeping at the sight of it—two grown men who never gave a second glance at art in their lives; my mom had that effect on people), I auctioned off everything else I could think of, rolling every penny into Michael's account.

Of course nothing was for me. Of course everything was for Michael. Because I'm my father's daughter. And I know how to protect my family.

The truancy officer arrived before the police did. He was a thin man with no chin to speak of. He covered his mouth with his hand when he spoke. The social worker came with him.

"I'm required to inform you I'm recording this interaction," she said cheerfully.

"I know," I said. "You don't have to tell me each time. Please come in."

They were both visibly surprised at being invited in so quickly. The truancy officer gasped a bit at the immaculate house. Every surface gleamed. I'm fairly certain it wasn't what he was expecting. He cleared his throat.

"Young lady," he began, "you haven't been in school for—" He checked his notes. "Good Lord. How have you missed these many days?"

"Where's your mother?" the social worker asked.

"I look after myself," I said. "And my brother. And . . ." I cued the waterworks. "No one can hurt us anymore." There was no stopping what was going to happen next, so I figured I would make it count.

The social worker took off her glasses, but she laid them on the table still facing me. The lights in the corners still shone like emeralds. She may have taken me for a fool, but that didn't mean I had to act like one. I wiped my eyes, keeping my face to the camera.

"I'll ask again," the social worker said. "Where is your mother?"

"Gone," I said. "With that man. The one who hurt her. She told us not to look for her. She told us that she wouldn't be coming back." I turned toward the window. "Sometimes, I feel like I can still hear them in the studio. She was screaming." I pulled in a shuddering breath. I cupped my hands over my face. I pretended to sob. "I wasn't supposed to tell."

I had practiced all of this. The adults looked at one another. And then they called the police.

Michael and I had to give statements. *Yes,* we explained. She had a lover who hit her. *No,* we added. We didn't know where he was. We didn't know where she had gone. We hoped she was okay.

That bloodstain? I said to the detective. *That was just a bird. He flew in and messed with the fibers. It panicked and smacked its body against the pillar and then the floor. It had no idea what it was doing, and continued to flail about even when it was bleeding. You know birds.*

The detective said that they would want to test it, just to make sure. They did. The lab said it wasn't human blood. "Some sort of bird," it said in the report. I almost wept in relief.

Collectors continued to hound us, even after everything was sold, scratching at our digital door like dogs. Asking if there was anything else, anything they could bid on. Unfinished projects. Notes on scratch paper. Journals, perhaps. Maybe a painting or a sculpture or a handmade sweater. People itched for her work.

"Enigmatic Artist Disappears into the Night, Leaves Children Behind," the newspapers headlined breathlessly. They reported that police had found her blood in her bedroom. On the wall. On the sheets. This was true, of course, and it was old. The crane was worse than I had thought. They said there was another bloodstain in the studio but neglected to mention that it was from a bird. They wrote maudlin pieces about her somber, large-eyed boy, now motherless in a cruel and unfeeling world. They didn't mention me.

Which was fine, actually. Michael was placed with a nice family in a nice city. I wrote him letters every week, but I don't know if he ever saw a single one. I never heard back. I was placed in a group home, but I didn't stay there long.

People wanted to know if I was like my mother. Was I a doomed artist, or incurably promiscuous, or poetically tragic? Or maybe I was all of those things at once. It was nothing I wanted to talk about. It was none of their business. Things were better when I took off and headed out on my own.

Eventually, Michael ran away from his foster family when he turned sixteen. Wrote them a note saying that he was going out to find our mom. He didn't mention me. I don't even know if he remembered me that well. I don't know what his foster family told him. He didn't bring anything with him when he left—not even a knapsack. He just disappeared into the night. No one has heard from him since. I check the balance of the account I set up for him every year, but so far he hasn't touched it. I don't know if he remembers that it's there.

That was ten years ago. Twenty years since Mom . . . well, I don't even know the word for it. Passed on? Crossed over? *Changed?* Mothers don't stay on the farm. They fly away. I don't know why I ever thought she would be any different. Even though there was no farm anymore to fly from. How can you run from your birthright when your birthright is gone?

Every month, I put messages on the internet, on library bulletin boards, in newspapers for whatever town I think maybe my brother might have gone to. Every time, it says the same thing: "Michael: Everything would have been fine if she just never met that crane. I'm here when you need me, buddy." So far, nothing. I still have hope, though.

I haven't been back to the farm. Or the farmhouse. No one owns the farm. The farm belongs to the corn. I have no interest in going back.

I work now painting people's portraits for money. Or painting portraits of their dogs, which weirdly pays more. It's not a lot, but I get by. I still draw pictures of my dad. I still haven't shown them to anyone. I live in the middle of the city, but it's strange how many sounds remind me of the farmhouse. The voices of drunks stumbling out of the bar at night is eerily similar to the bellows of our sheep. The hum of traffic on the interstate is a dead ringer for the sound of drones. Every time an old beater starts up I rush to the window to look for the plows. And every time I hear the hiss of the electric wires running through the alley outside my apartment, I could swear I was hearing the sound that the corn makes as it grows.

Maybe we never actually run away. Maybe everywhere's the same.

Every once in a while, a crane lights on my window. She stares at my easel. She stares at my paints. She stares at the loom that I built myself and my first attempts at weaving. Because of course I would teach myself to weave. You can take the girl off the farm, but you can't take weaving out of a weaver. I guess we really are what we're born for.

The crane presses her body against the glass. She is a

beautiful thing—startlingly white feathers, an elegant beak, and a supple grace to her movements. I notice that today she has a deep gash over one eye. A bit of blood staining the fluff on her rump. It's not the first time she's come to me injured. I try not to look at her. She taps my window, again and again.

I could help you, you know, she seems to say, her eye finding the partially woven cloth on the loom.

"I don't need any help," I say out loud. I return to my work. The crane remains on the windowsill, her long neck stretching sweetly forward. She tilts her head. Her black eye is a pool of ink. It is a bottomless pit. It is a collapsed star, all density and hunger and relentless gravity, pulling everything it can into its center—to be unraveled, unmade, undone, and unrecognizable. How can anyone survive that kind of love?

Art exists to transcend, transfix, and transform. She taps the glass with growing insistence.

"So I've been told," I say without looking up.

I could make it beautiful. I could make everything beautiful. Art could change your life. Art could give you wings. And you could fly away. Don't you want to fly away?

I wonder if she knows it's a lie. I don't get up. I don't engage. I make my own art. At my loom I add stitches to a piece I've been working on. A small boy running through a field of corn, in pursuit of a bird, a bright red button stitched over his heart. I knot the thread and pull it tight.

Acknowledgments

I wrote this book in an ancient RV, purchased on a farm in southern Minnesota. The widow selling it explained that the land had been in her family for a long time, but it was about to be sold and the old farmhouse razed to make room for more corn. "Seems strange not to live on the land you cultivate," she said as we signed the purchase papers for the vehicle that we hoped would be sound enough to carry our family across several states. "Seems strange to sell your family's legacy to a person who's not a person at all." I agreed, but what can you do? The world changes, after all.

I wrote this story largely by accident. We were deep in the pandemic and driving our still-unvaccinated oldest child to college. It was an anxious time. We took a wide, scenic loop, avoiding crowds, and traveled along pretty country roads dotted with abandoned farm buildings, corn and soybeans stretching all the way to the sky. Somewhere in Indiana, I caught my breath at the sight of a crane, standing on the roof beam of a collapsing house. I don't know why he transfixed me so, and I don't know why he chose to bide his time on that particular sagging roof—a tenacious king of a domain slumping towards ruin. Awash as I was with thoughts of dissolution and despair, of altered norms and fraying social fabrics, of persisting and surviving—and how we survive our own survival—I opened up my computer, and in walked that crane.

This story would not have become what it is now without the gentle questions and boundless positivity of Jonathan Strahan—if I challenge you to find a nicer editor, I assure you that you will not win. Also crucial—the incisive critiques of my writing group, the Wyrdsmiths (Lyda Morehouse, Naomi Kritzer, Theo Lorenz, Adam Stemple, and Eleanor Arnason), as well as my other readers (cheerleaders?): Laura Ruby, Martha Brockenbrough, Olugbemisola Rhuday-Perkovich, Laurel Snyder, Tracey Baptiste, Linda Urban, and Kate Messner. Writing is a solitary pursuit, except when it is not. And where would any of this be without Steve Malk, both agent and champion, who really puts up with a lot, if I'm being honest. My career exists because of you, Steve. Thanks for everything.